Waiting To Wake

by Mary DeRosa Hughes

Thank You, Mom.

"Love is so short, forgetting is so long."

- Pablo Neruda

Chapter One

"Are you ready to see her?"

Rob and I have been sitting in the hospice lobby for fifteen minutes before the nurse, whose tag shows her name is Rebecca, arrives to take us back to my mom's room. I stand up and look back at my husband, who is rooted to his seat, his eyes avoiding mine by fixating on some mysterious spot on the floor. I put my hand on his shoulder, a gentle nudge toward what we know has to be done. He gives me a flicker of a glance before his gaze goes back to the tiles.

"You need a moment?" Rebecca asks, obviously well-versed in the scenario that she's watching unfold before her. I nod, and she moves away just out of earshot.

"What's wrong?" I whisper.

"I told you, I hate hospitals," Rob says. "They freak me out."

"This is a *hospice*, not a hospital," I remind him.

"At least patients have a chance of leaving a hospital," Rob says. His eyes widen as mine start to burn.

"Shit. I'm sorry, Char... I didn't mean..." He drops his head into his hands, exhaling a gust of frustration.

Rob's father passed away unexpectedly last year. A massive heart attack while he was tooling around the eighteenth hole with his cronies at the golf club. Rob was devastated, but even in his grief, he said more than once that he was glad that his dad went the way that he did: mercifully fast and doing something that he loved.

As I sit there watching Rob battle the urge to flee, I look up to see a beautifully familiar face coming toward me: my mom's best friend, Jana.

"I didn't know you were here," I say, as she envelops me in a hug. "But I'm so glad you are."

"You, too, honey," she says. "Just took a minute to grab some coffee. Got here at six this morning and I can't seem to clear the cobwebs."

"Me neither." I glance over at Rob, who looks up from the floor long just enough to acknowledge Jana with a nod and a faint smile.

I understand him not wanting to see my mom like this. I don't want to, either. But right now, it's not about my discomfort, sadness, or anything else except the fact that she needs me. And I need her, too.

Jana takes a sip of her coffee. "There's something I have for you," she says. "I meant to bring it with me, but… well, I'm just really scattered this morning. But I'll get it to you soon."

I start to ask what it is, but I see Rebecca out of the corner of my eye approaching cautiously. She puts her hand gently on my shoulder and asks again if we're ready to see my mother. I don't answer for a moment, trying to gauge Rob's reaction, which consists of a look that says, "I'm sorry, but…"

"Go on, honey," Jana says. "I'll stay with him."

So, I go in to see Mom alone.

*

I enter the room and see her propped up on her bed by a pile of soft pillows, her legs covered with a colorful quilt that looks like someone's grandma made it. Her eyes are closed, and she seems to be lightly napping.

"She's not in any pain," Rebecca assures me. "We've made sure of that."

"Good. Thank you. I… is she…" I stumble, trying to choose which of the ten thousand questions I have to ask next. Thankfully, Rebecca reads my mind.

"She's heavily medicated, but still cognizant," Rebecca says. "At least most of the time. There will be moments when she'll be talking to me, or one of the other nurses, about something, and then she'll just… drift."

"*Drift?*"

"That's my word for it," Rebecca says, giving a slight smile. "Her gaze will sort of move past you as if she sees someone far more interesting across the room. And then she'll start talking softly, usually in words I can't understand."

"Is that normal?" I ask.

"I'm sure some of it is due to the medication," Rebecca says. "But really, there is no such thing as 'normal' in a situation like this. In the fifteen years

I've been here, I have yet to see two people prepare to transition exactly the same way."

I nod, willing my eyes not to fill up. Rebecca puts her hand on my shoulder and gives it a little squeeze. "How about I give you two some time? I'll be right down the hall if you need me."

Rebecca leaves, the door swooshing shut behind her. I tread softly across the floor to the bed, trying not to wake Mom even though I want so much for us to talk.

My mother, Beth Reade, age sixty-eight, is dying. I know this is reality, but looking at her right now, I can't see a cancer patient. Even after five years of off-and-on chemo and a twenty-pound weight loss from her already slender frame, she still radiates an almost patrician beauty that makes death seem like it's decades—not days—away. I remember her friends always called her "Grace"—as in Grace Kelly. They weren't wrong.

I start to reach for Mom's hand but find myself easing onto the bed next to her instead. She stirs as I nestle close.

"Just like when you were a little girl; always finding an excuse to share the bed with me," she laughs softly. "I guess this is about the best reason yet, huh?"

I want to say something cute in response, but I just nod, feeling my eyes grow hot and damp again. I mentally grab myself by the shoulders, trying to shake out the need to collapse in a puddle. The last thing I want is for her to feel like she can't let go of this life because I can't handle it.

"Is Rob here with you?" she asks.

"Yeah, he's… um… in the lobby," I stammer. "It's not that he doesn't care. Honestly, that's not it. I think he's just… he gets all weirded out in hospitals. I know this isn't a *hospital*, but still…"

Mercifully, she cuts me off with a wave of her hand. "Men. We always think they're supposed to be the strong ones, the saviors. And maybe that's not fair. Because sometimes they just *can't* be there for us," she says, shaking her head. "In spite of their best intentions."

She goes silent for a long moment, fiddling with what she always called her 'right-hand ring': a thin rose gold band inlaid with tiny diamonds. She's worn it for as long as I can remember, having long since outlasted the wedding set that came off when my parents divorced decades ago. It spins too easily around on her finger, and I catch myself thinking I should get it sized for her.

"Are you okay?" I ask, worried that she's hurt by Rob waiting in the lobby.

She looks up from her hand and answers my question with one of her own. "Are you happy, sweet girl?"

"I'm not really sure I can wrap my head around the concept of happiness right now, Mom."

"I don't mean with *this*," she says, gesturing to the array of meds and machines next to her bed. "I mean with your life."

"Sure. Things are good."

"*Things*? For a writer, you could certainly use some help with eloquence," she says, giving me a wink. "You *are* still writing, aren't you?"

"Sure," I say, feeling the slow tide of guilt rising in my chest. The truth is, I haven't written a word in six months. "The firm has been crazy-busy, so I don't get to do as much of it as I'd like."

"But you're not giving up," she says.

"No, I'm not," I say, feeling more and more like a fraud. Actually, I think of giving up every time I sit down to write. Or every time another twenty-something wunderkind bursts onto the literary scene in a shower of accolades as I approach my forty-fifth year on the planet.

"Good," she says. "Don't ever let your job get in the way of your work."

"I won't," I promise, knowing I've done exactly that.

"You still haven't answered my first question."

"Huh?"

"Charlotte Elizabeth, *really…*"

"Mom, please stop worrying about me," I say. "Okay, yes. I'm happy."

"I hope so," she says, wincing slightly as she readjusts her position on the bed. "I really do." She reaches for what looks like a television remote and clicks a little blue button in the center. The pain pump hums in response, and she visibly relaxes.

I reach out to stroke her hair. It came back after the chemo curlier and flecked with gray that was never there before the cancer. She was happy about the curls; not so much about the silver sparkles. I feel like we should be talking, but I can't think of anything to say except that I love her. So, I do.

"I love you, too, hon," she says, removing the delicate band from her finger and slipping it onto mine. "More than anyone in this world or the next."

As I look down at her ring on my hand, a sob escapes from me that is so loud I'm afraid it'll bring the entire hospice staff running. *Hold it together, Char. She doesn't need this.*

But as I swipe my shirtsleeve across my face, mopping up tears the way I did when I was five, I notice that Mom isn't put off by the outburst. She's looking past me as if I'm not there at all.

Drifting.

She starts humming to herself, with a hint of a smile on her face. I start to reach for the call button to summon Rebecca, but my mother looks so content that I don't want to disturb whatever peace she's found in this moment.

"Mom?" I whisper. "Are you with me? I… I don't know what to do. If you need to go, it's okay. I swear, I'll be fine…" The tears are coming again, but I'm past caring about decorum.

I start to tell her again how much I love her, how much I'll miss her… but she's now added some words to the little tune she's singing to herself. I try to make them out, but I can't.

"What?" I ask, feeling panicky even though Rebecca said Mom would slip in and out of consciousness and say things that made no sense.

For just a few seconds her eyes focus on me with a laser-like clarity, even as she continues with the singsong phrase I can just now barely decipher.

"Just like the whiskey… just like the whiskey…"

"Mom, what are you saying? I don't understand…"

And then she gives me the most beautiful smile. And she is gone.

*

I'm vaguely aware that Father Brian is reciting something biblical as I stand here on Mom's favorite beach cove, surrounded by a small coterie of people who loved her. I feel multiple eyes, Rob's included, turning discreetly in my direction, watching for signs of an imminent meltdown. But there won't be much of a show because all I can do is stare at the small box of remains resting in my hands; trying to grasp that this mix of soft, grayish cinders and tiny white bits that remind me of crushed seashells was once my mother.

"Char… I think it's almost time," Rob says. He sounds nervous like I might turn around and slap him. He slips his arm around my waist, trying to offer now what we both know I needed a week ago in the hospice. I tense involuntarily, and he feels it.

"It's a time for soft words and strong hugs," Father Brian continues. "It's a time for supporting one another in the midst of our sadness and our grief. So, I thank you all for being here, for remembering Beth…"

I can tell that his pastoral spiel is winding down, and I feel my heart start to a pound like a jackhammer. In just a moment, I'm going to be expected to lead everyone down to the shoreline and release Mom's ashes into the sea.

But I can't. I don't want to. It's all I have left of her.

Father Brian has finished, and the crowd is starting to murmur, waiting for me to take the first step toward the water. I feel Rob start to move forward, his forearm putting light pressure on my back. I know people are staring at me, and that it's making my husband hugely uncomfortable. I root my feet more deeply into the sand and grip the box tighter.

"Come on, it'll be okay," Rob says, trying to coax me forward. I start to speak so quietly that he has no choice but to stop and lean close to hear me.

"This isn't like your Dad, okay?" I say. "From the day she was diagnosed until the day she died two years later, I have had to let her go in pieces. This is the last one. Please don't rush me."

As Rob backs away, I see Jana coming toward me. Before I can say a word, she hugs me to her chest and plants a kiss on the top of my head.

"The ocean will wait," Jana whispers. "The waves aren't going anywhere. And neither am I."

I feel my heart begin to slow, the anxious gripping in my chest replaced by tears of release. When I finally move several moments later, everyone follows along in silence, padding through the sand until it becomes wet under our feet. Father Brian asks if I want to say anything, and I shake my head no. But Jana steps forward, pulls a folded piece of paper from her pocket, and begins to read aloud. As I wade out into the ocean with Mom's remains, I hear Jana saying her own goodbye in a hushed and broken tone.

"You lived from the inside out, holding each day in your heart. Who you were, what you were, how you were… our lives needed you to erase well-rehearsed routines. We will miss your heart that loved, your eyes that smiled, your ears that listened, your touch that warmed and your words that made us laugh.

"Full sails, Beth… go with God."

Chapter Two

We're pulling up in front of my Aunt Fran's house, and it looks like most everyone has arrived before us. I can't stand my aunt's house. It's dark, dusty, and always smells like reheated meatloaf and cheap potpourri. Jana had wanted to have the reception at her place, but it was just too small for so many people. So, here we are at the mausoleum.

I grab my purse and try to will myself to get out of the car. But instead, I just sit there while Rob rummages in the back seat for a box of cookies that we bought from the bakery on the way here. I can see through Fran's front window that it's a full house, and I'm happy that people appear to be smiling and chatting as they remember Mom, rather than standing around grim-faced and sobbing. But no matter how warm and welcoming the crowd looks, I'm still not ready for this.

"Char, come on. Let's go." Rob is standing on the passenger side, staring at me through the glass. I try to take a deep breath, but my lungs won't accept more than a small gulp of air. He opens my door and extends his hand to help me out of the car.

"I'll be there in a minute."

He starts to say something, but I can see him doing a mental replay of our ash scattering standoff earlier this morning. He clears his throat, gives me an *okay, you win* nod and begins heading toward the house.

As he walks away, a crushing hollowness settles in my chest that I wish I could attribute solely to missing my mother. But the truth is, I miss my husband, too. The Rob I married would have sat out here with me for hours, not caring if anyone thought it was inappropriate for the daughter of the deceased to refuse to come inside and mingle over hors d'oeuvres. *We're our own family now*, he'd remind me. Just like he did on our wedding day seventeen years ago.

I'm sure Rob would argue that the Charlotte he signed up for wouldn't have frozen him out when he tried making up for his blunder. She would have applauded his effort rather than measuring how extensive and well executed it was. Forgiveness would have come in minutes, not months. *That* Charlotte would have felt the first tiny fissure of disconnect and mended it before it widened into the chasm that seems to have become our new normal.

I can see my Aunt Fran peering out at me through the window, her face pinched. After a moment, Rob comes up behind her, puts his hands on her shoulders and whispers something in her ear. Whatever he's saying, it's not having a soothing effect. Fran turns toward him and begins alternately flailing her arms and pointing in my direction as Rob, ever the diplomat, nods his head in agreement with whatever she's bitching about. And I'm pretty sure it's me, and my horrid lack of respect for her sister. Never mind that she and Mom were never close. To her, this reception is just another cocktail party with mourners thrown in for atmosphere. And I'm blowing the curve by not playing the part of the grieving daughter as scripted. With Fran, it's all about appearances.

So, I guess it's time for me to appear.

*

Slipping in the front door, I take a quick scan of the room. The place is full of people I've never seen before in my life, and that's actually sort of comforting. It'll buy me a few moments of anonymity while I seek out the person I want to see the most: Jana. She's the closest thing I have to a mother, and right now I just want to sink into her arms like an infant.

"Praise the good Lord, you're here!"

Before I can say a word, Fran has grabbed me in a hug that feels more like a quarterback sack than an embrace. As I try to gracefully extricate myself, she breaks into a crescendo of overwrought, dry-eyed sobs. Several people turn in our direction and give us pitying looks, playing perfectly into Fran's grieving sibling schtick.

"Are you okay, sweetheart?" she says, trapping my face between her palms. I can smell her fake lavender scented hand cream, and it's making me nauseous.

"I'm fine, Fran," I whisper, trying to deflect the attention she's intent on drawing to us.

"Oh, darling, you don't have to act so strong!" she booms out, clutching at the giant silver cross dangling from her neck. "I'm here for you."

Just like you were for Mom, right? I think, recoiling inwardly. *You'd go to church and throw out a pious prayer for her in front of your ladies group, but God forbid you'd come by the house. That's no surprise, though, is it? You always envied your sister. Her beauty, her class… everything about her. Wait, isn't envy one of the seven deadly sins? I'd like to take that rosary of yours and…*

"Hey, hon, Rob's been looking all over for you."

It's my best friend, Abby, coming to my rescue. I guess God has forgiven me for my evil fantasy of strangling Fran with her holy jewelry.

"And your Dad's here, too," Abby continues, taking my arm and gently pulling me toward her. "Did you know he was coming?"

I shake my head, then turn back to Fran. "I'd better go. We'll catch up later, okay?"

Realizing that her performance is over, Fran nods, pats me on the shoulder and heads toward the back bedroom. I watch as several other old biddies follow in her wake, chattering amongst themselves.

"Thank you for saving me," I say as we begin weaving through the crowd. "It's hard enough being here without watching her chew the scenery."

"No shit," Abby says, rolling her eyes. "I can't even believe that sanctimonious lunatic is related to Beth. Your mom was the real deal. Not a pretentious bone in that gorgeous bod of hers."

I nod, feeling hot tears pooling behind my eyes. I blink them back as we approach Rob, who is chatting with my father in a far corner of the room.

"Hi, babe," Rob says, pulling me close to him. This time, I don't stiffen at his touch.

"I didn't know you'd be here," I say to my father.

"I was going to just send flowers, but Alice said I should bring them in person," Dad replies, motioning toward an elaborate arrangement sitting on a table near the buffet. *The first time he's ever brought Mom flowers, and she's not here to enjoy them.*

"They're lovely," I say. "Be sure to thank Alice for me." Alice is my Dad's second wife. They married not long after he and Mom split and started their own family right away. I saw Dad less and less often in the years following.

"I… just wanted to make sure you were okay. I'm… ah…" Dad stammers. It's painful to watch him grasp for words that don't come naturally to him. Ones like, *I'm sorry,* and *I love you.*

"I'm going to get a drink," Rob interjects. "Do either of you want anything?" We both shake our heads, and Rob disappears.

"So, how are the boys?" I ask, referring to my two half-brothers that I barely know.

"Not really boys anymore," Dad says, laughing softly. "David is twenty-nine, and Marcus just turned thirty-two. He and his wife are expecting a baby in a few months."

"Wow. So, you're gonna be a grandpa. Congratulations."

"Thanks. Alice can't stop buying clothes for the little rug rat," Dad says, shaking his head with a faint smile.

"I can't blame her," I say. "Mom always hoped Rob and I would have kids. But we're happy with the four-legged variety." I'm talking about Phoebe, our "mystery mix" mutt that we adopted five years ago. She is the love of my life and works this to her every advantage.

"Your mother would have been an excellent grandma," he says, his eyes softening. "You know I always cared for her, even after she left. I never would've wished for this…"

"It's all right. I know." I start to initiate an awkward hug, but his eyes are now looking past me. I follow his gaze and see Jana mingling in the crowd.

"I think I'm gonna go," he says, giving me a quick squeeze. "Say hello to Jana for me. I know she's got to be crushed. She and Beth were inseparable."

"I'll let her know you're thinking of her."

He moves toward the door, then stops and begins talking again without fully turning back to face me.

"Look… I know we don't see each other much. And I've been mostly to blame for that," he murmurs. "But I'm always here for you, okay?"

"Thanks," I say, meaning it. "I'll remember that."

As I watch him walk away, Rob shows up, drink in hand. "Where'd your dad go?"

"Home," I say. Across the room I see Jana heading toward the kitchen with a stack of empty serving trays. "Look, I'm gonna go talk to Jana. Do you mind?" Rob nods okay, and I head off.

The kitchen is mercifully free of anyone but Jana, who is artfully arranging a platter of canapes that would have looked delicious to me if my stomach weren't in knots.

"I should've known you made the food. It's all gorgeous," I say. "But I guarantee you Fran is out there taking credit for everything."

"I don't give a rat's ass," Jana says, her voice cracking slightly. "This is for Beth, not that uptight old bat."

I start to comment, but Fran appears in the doorway, eyes narrowed and darting back and forth between us.

"Charlotte, everyone is asking about you. Why don't you stop hiding in the kitchen and be gracious enough to come say hello?"

"I've been in here for five seconds," I say. "I'll be out in a bit."

"Don't be long." Fran gives me a look of disgust and stomps away, her fat old lady heels clopping on the tiles. I close my eyes, willing the angry tears that want to spill down my face to go away. Jana pulls me into the hug I've needed since I got here.

"Don't let her get to you," she whispers.

"It's not even about her," I say. "I'm just so fucking tired, sad, and… just *everything*. I can't explain it."

"You don't have to," Jana says, releasing me so she can wipe away her own tears. "I've been all over the emotional map, too. I wish I had the words to express how much your mom meant to me."

"You did," I say. "The eulogy you gave was beautiful. I had no idea you could write like that."

"That means a lot coming from you," Jana says, giving me a tiny smile. "You're a wonderful writer. Always have been, since you were a little girl."

"Well, if I ever had any wordsmith mojo, it's definitely left the building," I say.

"It'll come back," Jana says. "You've got so much on your mind right now."

"I know. But, to be honest, I felt this way even before Mom got sick," I say. "Whatever I start just falls flat. It's like I can't find anything that's worth writing about. Something that really *matters* to me."

Jana gives me a long look. "I think I have something that might help," she says. "It's what I meant to give to you at the hospice, but I brought it with me today. Let's take a break from catering duty and go get it out of my car."

"What is it?" I ask, trailing after Jana as moves to grab her keys. She is about to answer, but instead nearly collides with Fran who is marching back into the kitchen to ferret me out.

Before Fran can say a word, Jana begins speaking directly to me as if my aunt isn't even there.

"What I have for you… you'll want to spend some time alone with it. Away from prying eyes," she says, shooting Fran a pointed glare. "Come to my house Saturday morning for coffee. I'll give it to you then."

Chapter Three

"Welcome back, Charlotte. How are you feeling?" Trina, the practice manager here at Steiner Chase & Associates, asks in the gentle tone she probably uses with her three small children.

"I'm doing okay."

"Well, if you need anything, don't hesitate to ask." She pats my arm reassuringly, but I can tell she's trying to figure out how to segue from empathetic chatter into workaday issues.

"Thanks, Trina." I look around my uncharacteristically neat desk, which has obviously been tidied in my absence. "So, what sort of family law festivities are on tap for today?"

She brightens, eager to fill me in on what the day ahead holds, as well as all the fun I missed while I was gone. She scoots me out of the way, plops into my seat and pulls up the daily schedule on my desktop.

"Hmmm… looks like we've got Jill Keller first up at 9:00. You remember her? She came in for a free divorce consult about six months ago, then decided she wanted to give things another try—say it with me—'for the children.' But apparently, even four kids aren't enough to help her get past finding Mr. Keller humping away on top of the nanny last week."

"You'd think these guys would get a little more creative in their adulterous choices. The nanny? Please. That's so played out."

"I know, right?" Trina shrieks. She scans the calendar again, clearly hoping to find a full roster of crazy.

By the almost joyful look on her face, she isn't disappointed. God, I wish I could mainline whatever she's drinking so I could love my job the way she loves hers.

"Okay, the O'Neals are coming by at 10:00 to sign legal separation papers. Amicably. Yawn." But her displeasure at seeing a drama-free appointment on the agenda is short-lived, and she breaks into a satisfied smile. "But right after that, we've got 'Doctor Love.' Sweet!"

"Who?" I'm beginning to regret having asked for her take on today's lineup.

"You haven't met him yet. He hired us the day after you left. Anyway, his actual name is Dr. Lovell. He's a totally hot neurosurgeon, and he's divorcing his crazy bitch of a wife."

I'm really ready for Trina to vacate my desk so I can get to the business of numbing myself with data entry and paper shuffling. But she is not going anywhere until I allow her to offer at least a few morsels of the spousal lunacy this poor, genetically-blessed neurosurgeon has been forced to endure.

"So, just exactly how batshit is she?"

"Well, she's clearly studied the *Fatal Attraction* playbook. Some garden-variety car vandalization, stalking him at work. Thankfully, no bunny boiling. But she did take the liberty of filling his entire collection of designer shoes with dog shit."

Trina is just about to launch into further details of this decidedly unholy union when Erica Steiner strides through the front door in all her Amazonian glory. She is probably six feet tall in her designer heels, with a mane of honey blonde hair and a ridiculously perfect spa glow. She is also one of the top attorneys in Southern California, with a well-earned reputation for stomping opposing counsel into a puddle in the courtroom.

"Char, you're back!" Litigation Barbie exclaims cheerfully, almost as if I'd been on a Tahitian vacation instead of attending my mother's funeral.

"Yep. Trina's been filling me in on everything that's been happening around here."

"Great. Well, we've got a shitload of things going on today. Trina, I need you to come and help Denise with the exhibits for the Weiland case. She's been trying to Bates stamp all of them herself, and I think she's going to stroke out. And that can't happen. At least not until opposing counsel gets their file box full of fuck-you docs before three o'clock today." Erica turns her attention back to me with a look of grave importance.

"Please tell me we have coffee."

*

After completing the vital task of brewing a giant pot of caffeine, I'm parked back at the front desk, entering the time sheets that everyone at the firm keeps.

13

Everything from phone calls to glancing in the general direction of a case file is considered billable time and failing to record even one precious second of it is tantamount to treason.

I'm not even twenty minutes into this data entry festival and I'm already jonesing for a break. So, with no clients in the waiting area and everyone else ensconced in their own circle of legal hell, I pull a thumb drive out of my purse and slip it into the desktop. While that syncs up, I open a few work-related documents I can jump to, if need be. I look around one more time, then open up the story I've been toying with. It's actually not a story quite yet; just a tangle of thoughts that recur almost daily since Mom passed.

You are *still writing, aren't you?*

I close my eyes for a split second, savoring the sound of her voice one more time. And then I begin.

*

"What's that you're working on?"

I spin around in my chair to find Denise, Erica's paralegal, peering over my shoulder at the document that is decidedly not the Consent Decree that I'm supposed to be editing. I shrink the page down, silently cursing myself.

"I'm just taking a break," I say, attempting a clipped tone that suggests it's no big deal that she just saw me screwing off on company time. I fail miserably, my voice rising one panicky octave too many.

"So, you're a writer?" I can't tell if she's really interested or just mocking me.

"Yeah, I guess. I mean, it's just something I've done all my life. I love it."

"And that's why you're working here." Yep, definitely mocking.

"It's called paying the bills." I turn away and continue pounding on the keys, hoping Denise will vaporize.

Instead, she strolls around to the front of my desk, so she's dead center in my field of vision. I'm surprised to see her face has softened slightly from scorn into what looks like some sort of quasi-empathy.

"That's what it all comes down to, right?" I nod in agreement, if only to get her to overlook my wannabe Hemingway moment. I don't need Erica burying one of her Louboutins between my shoulder blades for insubordination.

"I sure didn't think I'd be doing this for over twenty years," she continues.

Denise is about my age, so I do the math and figure she probably landed in the legal world in her early twenties. "So, what did you do before this?"

"Went to art school. Tended bar. Had fun. Why not? I was a kid." She rolls her eyes and gives a derisive snort. "At least I was until I had one."

"Yeah, I'm sure that was a game changer."

"No shit. Autumn's dad ran off after the first few diaper changes, so guess who had to keep the lights on?"

I give her a tense smile and bob my head up and down again, grateful that the subject has shifted away from me.

"I made good money at the bar, but I couldn't be working all night with a baby at home. So, I quit slinging drinks, dropped out of art school and got my paralegal certificate." She looks away and begins fiddling with a paper clip. "It's not like anyone was exactly heralding me as the next Cezanne."

"You still paint?" I ask. "I'd love to see some of your work." I am actually not bullshitting her. It would be fascinating to see physical proof that Denise still has a little slice of her soul left for herself.

Instead, she looks at me like I'm certifiable. "Are you kidding me? All I want to do when I get home is pass out on the couch, not whip out a canvas and make a god-awful mess."

"Well, I still think it's an amazing talent to have," I offer.

"That's nice of you to say," Denise says in a flat tone that signals she's ready to stick a fork in this conversation. "But what's the point of doing something if you'll never get paid for it? All this 'for the love of the craft' stuff is complete crap." She motions toward my computer screen with a sardonic chuckle as she turns to head back to her desk.

"You of all people should know that."

As Denise saunters away, I feel my relief at our conversation having ended replaced by a simmering fury. At first I think it's directed at Denise for her pronouncement that my pursuit of writing is just an embarrassing lark. But then I realize the person I'm angry with is *me*. My crabby co-worker was simply voicing the toxic sentiment that I've been quietly feeding on for decades.

I close my document, fire up a search engine and type in the three words that I pray will serve as a long-overdue boot in the ass: *local writers groups*.

A long list comes up, and I scan it quickly, looking for anything close to home. But one group in particular jumps out at me, and I jot it down on a sticky note, smiling at the name.

Scribe Tribe.

Chapter Four

"I'm so sorry about your mom, Char," says Will as he reaches across the table, patting my hand gently. "But I'm really glad you're back. I… *we* all missed you."

Will Kenter is the firm's accountant. We've been good friends for years now, ever since Trina assigned me to be his personal slave during the monthly invoicing onslaught. Actually, he's about the furthest thing from a tyrant there is, having been known to send me home at the end of an eleven-hour day and finish up my drudge work himself. He says it's for purely selfish reasons; namely a vested interest in preventing burnout, so I don't quit or drop dead before the next billing cycle.

"Thanks. I wish I could tell you I'm happy to be back, but…" I say, absently poking at my salad. It was nice of him to invite me to lunch, but my appetite is shot.

"You really should eat something," he says.

"I'm not hungry," I say. "May as well use this grief to get into my skinny jeans."

Will shakes his head and points to my plate. "*Mangia.*"

I roll my eyes and spear a chunk of lettuce to humor him. But his fussing is actually kind of sweet.

"So, Trina gave me the scoop on all the client craziness that went down while I was gone. What sort of mayhem did I miss in the wonderful world of bean counting?"

"Not much. Unless you count a balance sheet discussion with Erica that ended in a broken coffee mug and me choking down three painkillers for lunch."

I lean closer, scouring his features with mock concern. "Hmmm… no visible wounds. I'm guessing the wall was on the receiving end of said mug?"

"Lucky for me. This face is my fortune."

"Idiot." I smile in spite of myself.

"So, you want to talk mayhem," Will says, toying with one of the fries on his plate. "I'd say most of mine resides on the home front these days."

"Well, you've got a house full of teenage boys, right? Par for the course."

"It's not the kids," he says, pulling off his glasses and rubbing his eyes. "It's Shelly."

"What's wrong? Is she okay?"

"She's fine, I guess. Me? Not so much." He pauses, weighing his next words. "I'm just not sure I can live with her anymore."

Will has never said much about his wife, preferring instead to brag about his sons when it comes to family chit-chat. So, I'm more than a little surprised that he's suddenly lobbing this grenade of marital discontent.

"Maybe you're just hitting a rough patch. I mean, every relationship goes through ups and downs," I say.

"Thanks, Dr. Phil. Got any other gems for me?"

"Sorry. Master of the obvious."

"No worries," Will says, cracking a tiny smile. "What else do I expect you to say? You've been married a long time, too. What, twenty years?"

"Seventeen. Almost eighteen."

"Impressive," Will says, in a tone that makes him sound like he's evaluating a cash flow statement. "And you're happy?"

I nod, wondering where this is going. "So, what's happening with you and Shelly?"

Will doesn't answer right away, staring down into his iced tea. When he finally meets my gaze, his eyes are clouded with discontent.

"*Nothing* is going on. And that's the problem."

I wait for him to elaborate, but he just stares at me as if I'm supposed to instinctively know what constitutes the mysterious void between him and his wife.

"Never mind. I shouldn't have brought it up," Will says.

"But you did," I say. "So, it's obviously bugging you."

"Yeah. More than it used to," he says. "But the thing is, we've been just… I don't know, *orbiting* around each other for so long. It would feel weird to all of a sudden try being close again."

"I think she'd appreciate you wanting to rekindle the spark," I say.

"That would presume there was one, to begin with." I look for some glint of humor in his eyes, but he's not joking.

"Come on, you mean to tell me you married someone you weren't attracted to?"

"Oh sure, there was chemistry when we first started dating," Will admits. "She got pregnant our second month together."

"On purpose?" I say. "Sorry… I didn't mean it like that…"

"Well, it wasn't planned," Will says. "At least not by me."

"But you married her anyway." *Good one, Char.* "I mean, you felt it was the right thing to do."

"I suppose," he says. "I know it was probably a stupidly old-fashioned move. But I didn't want to be an every-other-weekend-and-holidays kind of dad. I had that growing up, and it sucked."

"Yeah, me too," I say, recalling my talk with Dad at the reception. "But once you had the kid, things got better for a while, right? I mean, you had two more."

"Look, it's not like we hated each other," he says. "Things were decent enough. Good job, nice house, great kids. Why rock the boat, you know?"

I nod, feeling my chest tighten. *Are you happy, sweet girl?*

"But the boys are growing up," he continues. "Pretty soon we won't have them as a buffer. It'll just be… *us*."

"And that scares you?"

"Big time. I'm ass-deep into my forties, and I can't see growing old with someone I feel so disconnected from," he says, shaking his head. "Listen to me. Midlife crisis much?"

"Well, until you buy a red Corvette and start cruising for Hooters waitresses, there's still hope."

"The funny thing is, I'm not even sure Shelly would notice if I drove the thing through the living room with some Playboy mansion refugee in my lap."

"Okay, now you're being ridiculous…"

"Actually, I'm not," he says. "As long as I bring home the money and keep her in full-time soccer mom status, she's good."

"But you're not," I say. "So, what do you want to do about it?"

Will rests his chin on his hand, the tiny furrow between his brows becoming more pronounced. I've seen this look at the office a million times: *I know the answer, but I'm not ready to reconcile with it yet.* So, he opts to answer my question with one of his own.

"How do you and Rob make it work?"

"If I say it's all about good communication and date nights, you'll just accuse me of channeling that self-help dipshit again."

"No, I won't. I swear." He reaches across the table again for my hand, but instead of a platonic pat, he holds onto it this time. "I really could use some advice."

"Look, I don't have the secret to a perfect marriage," I say, wondering if he's going to let go of my hand anytime soon.

"I don't need perfect," he says. "I just want someone I can talk to about more than carpool schedules and math tutors."

"I dunno. Math tutors are pretty riveting."

"And a sense of humor would be a huge bonus." The furrow is fading, and a smile pulls at the corners of his mouth. "I just wish…" he trails off, and I can see the hamster wheel that is his brain churning, editing himself before he continues.

"I wish she was more like you."

I casually untangle my hand from his and begin fishing for something—anything—in my purse. Not because I'm uncomfortable, but because I realize I'm feeling more at ease holding his hand than I should be.

"That's really sweet," I say as I apply the lip balm I dug out from the bottom of my bag. "Guess we should get back to the office. I'm still behind on a ton of things, and a death in the family only buys you so much leeway for overdue draft docs."

"Yeah, we probably should get going," Will says, waving down a passing server to get the check. "Let me settle up, and I'll meet you outside."

A few minutes later, Will emerges from the restaurant, and we head toward the car. He tries making conversation about what's waiting for us back at work, but there's a tinge of junior high school-style awkwardness floating in the air between us.

"Sorry if I weirded you out," he says. "I was just trying to say that it's nice to have a woman in my life—even if she's just a friend—who actually *gets* me. And if that's cheesy, shoot me. I'm an accountant, not a poet."

"It's not cheesy, and I refuse to shoot you," I say. "Offing the one person that keeps me sane in that nut house we're about to return to would be hugely unproductive."

"Glad you feel that way," Will says, giving me a relieved smile. I'm actually feeling relieved, too. Today's discussion was just a fluke. He just needed to vent about some typical suburban guy frustrations. I'm sure he has no intention of actually leaving his wife.

As Will starts up the car, his cell phone rings. He's got it synced to the car, so I can see on the display that it's Shelly calling. He doesn't answer, putting her straight through to voicemail and turning up the music on the radio.

Chapter Five

"It's so good to see you," Jana says as she hugs me at the door. "Come on in. I've got the coffee all brewed up."

I follow her into the kitchen where we usually hang out whenever I visit. Jana grabs two mugs and a box of Girl Scout cookies.

"You have to help me eat these," she commands as the coffee is poured. "Every year I get stuck buying boxes of these things from co-workers shilling for their kids. I think I'm going to start telling them I'm diabetic."

"If your office mates are anything like mine, that won't help." I shake my head and take a sip of the best cup of java I've had in a while. "They'd rather see me slamming insulin than have little precious not make her cookie quota."

Jana laughs. "So, how's work going?"

"Eh, it's going." I hate talking about work. "Best I can say is that it provides a ton of unintentionally great material. Bitter divorces, cheating, custody battles. Better than any soap opera."

"Then should I be expecting the next *Kramer vs. Kramer* from you?" I hate talking about writing even more. It just reminds me of how far I am from where I should be. I feel the familiar squeeze of regret coiling itself around my solar plexus.

"Doubtful," I say. "I live the drama eight hours a day, so spending even more time *writing* about it might put me over the edge."

"Or it could be therapeutic."

"I don't know," I say. "Maybe the most therapeutic thing I can do is to stop kidding myself."

"About what?" Jana prods.

"That someday I'll produce something worth publishing."

"Well, you'll never know until you finish that 'something' and let the world see it."

"Touché."

Jana puts her hand on my arm, giving it a gentle squeeze. "I'm not trying to pick on you," she says. "I just want to see you do what I know you're capable of."

"I started looking into some writers groups, and I think I found one," I say. "It's scary, but I know I've got to do it."

"Yes, you do," Jana says. "Sometimes when you get too far into your comfort zone, it stops being a comfort at all."

"Lemme guess. Oprah?"

"No," Jana grins. "Your mother."

Jana grabs the coffee pot and tops off both of our mugs. "Come on. Let me show you what you came here for."

I follow her down the hall, coffee in hand, to the guest bedroom. As warm and inviting as it looks, I feel a chill go through me. I grip my mug tighter and hold it close to my chest, hoping the heat will somehow thaw my insides.

"I know. It's hard for me to come in here, too," Jana says. I just nod and blink back more of the tears that seem to have their own agenda these days.

As I dab at my eyes, Jana reaches into the closet and pulls out a large rectangular box that's about half the size of the file boxes that line the walls of the firm. She places it on top of the comforter and waits for my reaction.

"Beth told me about this box the morning I visited her at the hospice, right before you got there," Jana says, clearing her throat a little.

I continue staring at the box, hesitant to touch it. Mom had written her name on the lid in her usual elegant cursive. Finally, I reach out to pick it up, and it's heavier than it looks.

"It's all of her mementos," Jana says. "Photos, books, journals… things like that. I didn't dig into it too much since it was meant for you."

"What did she say?"

"That she had planned to organize everything in the box… to 'make it pretty,' as she put it," Jana laughs softly and swipes at a stray tear as she sits down on the bed. "But that never happened. She didn't have much to leave you, but she wanted it all in order."

"Leave it to Mom to worry about something like that," I whisper, touching her ring on my right hand. "I'm just glad to have anything of hers at all." I put the box on the floor and join Jana on the bed.

"I know, honey," Jana says. "And I'm sure Beth does, too."

I nod in agreement, my mind roiling with the fresh ache of missing my mother, infused with the anxious anticipation over what I'll find once I delve into the memories she left behind.

*

I arrive home from Jana's and am relieved to see that Rob's car isn't in the garage. He's probably at the driving range hitting a bucket of balls. I really want some time alone to go through Mom's things, so I'm hoping he'll be gone for at least another hour or so.

Phoebe does her usual welcome dance when I come in, following me to the kitchen where I give her a treat. She flops down on the tile and crunches away while I put the box on the counter, take the lid off and peer inside. As Jana had said, it's filled to the top with photos and other personal keepsakes. There's so much there, I'm not even sure where to start. So, I just stand there until Phoebe interrupts my reverie by unceremoniously sitting on my foot.

"All right, all right," I say, tossing her another cookie before picking up the box and moving it to the kitchen table so I've got some room to spread out the contents. I reach inside and start removing things one by one. A thick pile of greeting cards tied together with ribbon and several smaller boxes filled with loose photos. A large empty album that was likely meant to house the aforementioned pictures as part of Mom's "make it pretty" project. At least a dozen, identical spiral bound notebooks like the ones she used to buy for me at the start of each school year.

Just underneath the notebooks, I see something that actually makes me smile in spite of myself: a well-worn copy of Erich Segal's *Love Story*. I remember Mom nestled with it in her favorite chair when I was a little kid, and not understanding why she read it if it made her cry. She tried explaining the idea of feeling sentimental, but as a comic book geek extraordinaire at the time, the concept was entirely lost on me. Whenever the movie version would play on television, Mom would sit glued to it, much to my father's dismay.

I start to thumb through the book, and see something wedged between two of the pages. My heart lodges somewhere near my throat when I realize what it is.

A photo of my mother planting a not even remotely platonic kiss on a man who is not even remotely my father.

Okay, so maybe this was before she met Dad. But I know that even as the thought bubbles up, it's a futile rationale. She had been with Dad since they were teenagers,

22

and she was easily in her thirties in this photo. Mid-thirties to be exact. Right around the age she was when she went back to work against my Dad's wishes, and things started to get shaky between them.

"The way your father acts, you'd think it was the 50s, not the 80s," she'd say to me whenever he'd grumble about her failure to find total fulfillment as a hausfrau. But I remember her being so excited to have landed a job at Encanto & Associates, one of the giants in the publishing industry. Even though she was "just a secretary," as my Dad frequently reminded her, Mom refused to feel anything but proud to be working in the world of literature, no matter how small her role.

My hands shaking, I flip the photo over. There it is, in her unmistakable script: *Me and Daniel at "Our Place"—Santa Barbara—September 1982.*

I swallow hard, the inside of my mouth turning to sand. Who is this Daniel guy? What was their "place?" My initial shock gives way to numbness as tendrils of memories from that time begin weaving themselves together: arguments behind closed doors, Mom spending less time at home, Dad sleeping in the guest room more often than not.

They were divorced exactly two years after this picture was taken.

*

After ten minutes I'm still standing there in the kitchen, unable to stop staring at the photo of Mom and Daniel. It feels almost like I'm invading something sacred, but I can't help myself. He's handsome in a sort of college professor kind of way and looks to be a good ten years older than her. My eyes roam over the scene, again and again, soaking in every nuance: the way her lips are joined with his, her body leaning in close; the fingers of his left hand gently entwined in her hair. The sense of sweet familiarity between them is palpable. *This was not a one-night stand.*

I glance at the clock on the microwave which tells me it's 3:45 pm. Or more accurately, given today's discovery, 5:00 somewhere. I grab a glass, pour some chardonnay, put everything back in the box and head toward the bedroom with it, Phoebe following in giddy pursuit. Nothing like a little day drinking after finding out your mother had an affair that was apparently the catalyst that pushed her marriage over the edge.

As I situate myself on the floor, my heart kicks up its tempo as I contemplate what else I'll find in the box. A part of me wants to devour every scrap of information Mom left behind. But that curiosity is countered by an equally strong push to slam the lid back on the box and throw it out in the garage. The sip of wine that I meant to take turns into a gulp as I reach once again for the photo of Mom and Daniel.

I knew growing up that my parents didn't have a perfect marriage. But I always figured they were just like so many other couples their age who liked each other well enough, had a kid or two, and carried on in some semblance of happiness for as long as they could. Then one day, lawyers were paid, paperwork shuffled, and possessions divided. Onward to the next great spousal adventure.

But that "next" didn't happen for my mother. It never made sense to me, because once word was out that Beth Reade was back on the market, an almost comical number of men barraged our house. Doctors, attorneys, wealthy executives and even a few of my father's friends all turned into half-witted school boys as they tried to woo her. Every now and then she'd let one of them take her out, but nothing ever progressed beyond a few dates. She didn't seem interested in letting any of them get too close and seeing her wrapped in Daniel's embrace makes it clear to me now as to why. No man was ever going to win her heart because it was already taken.

I grab one of her spiral notebooks from the box and leaf through the pages, which are filled with poetry snippets. Some of them are frequently quoted passages by well-known authors. But the vast majority of the verses written in my mother's hand are her own words. I read one aloud to myself:

I was waiting for your eyes to find me.
Going nowhere, searching.
I lived each day within itself.
Not even recognizing the emptiness inside me.
Then I met you.
And I realized that each day could be more beautiful than ever before.
It was a moment in time that I had dreamed of—and now it was real.
You must have known I was waiting.

I put down the notebook and reach for another. And then another. Each one is filled with poems about Daniel, and I can't help but wonder if she ever let him read any of them.

But the fact that she wrote them at all is what amazes me. When was the last time I wrote anything for Rob? Or even bought him a card and scribbled a quick *I love you* inside of it?

I honestly can't remember.

Chapter Six

"What's up with all this stuff?" Rob asks, gesturing to the assorted memorabilia scattered over the bedroom floor.

"It's a bunch of Mom's things," I say, reaching for a pile of notebooks. "I picked the box up from Jana today. I've barely gotten started going through all of it."

"Anything interesting?"

"Well…" I briefly consider telling him about Daniel, but it's too much, too soon. I haven't even digested it myself. "She wrote a lot. Some really beautiful poetry, actually. I never knew she was—"

"Really? That's cool," Rob says, cutting me off as he strips off his sweaty golf shirt. "Can you be ready to go in about an hour?"

"Ready to go where?" I ask, following him as he heads toward the master bathroom.

"Seriously, Char?" he says, turning on the shower. "You don't remember?"

"No, I don't. Wanna clue me in?"

"My company party. At the CEO's house." He turns off the shower and glares at me.

He's right. I completely forgot. "I'm sorry. It's just… I can't keep my head straight since Mom died," I say. "Maybe I should skip the party. You go and have a good time."

Rob inhales deeply, mentally counting to ten. I can feel him shift from combative to cajoling.

"I realize you're overwhelmed right now," he says, putting his hands on my shoulders and looking me in the eye. "And I'm not trying to force you into this."

"I know. But I just don't think I'm up for making cocktail chatter."

"It won't be for long. Just a few hours. I swear," Rob says, knowing that I know better. Once he gets around his cronies and begins holding court, it's a given that it'll be an all-nighter.

"Look, I'm just trying to not ruin your evening," I say. "I know this is a big deal. But it's not going to look great if your wife is standing around like some sort of zombie."

Rob takes his hands off my shoulders. Operation Cajole has now been aborted.

"What's *not* going to look great is the Director of Marketing showing up without his spouse," he says, folding his arms across his chest.

I look back toward the bedroom, wishing I could just spend a quiet evening reading more of Mom's poetry. Rob stares at me, waiting for my answer.

"All right," I say. "But my heart really isn't in this at all."

"It'll be good for you to get out of the house. Take your mind off of things," Rob says, relief saturating his voice. "Can you wear the red dress I got you for your birthday?" Without even waiting for my answer, he turns the shower on again and continues undressing.

I can't tell if he honestly believes that a cocktail party is appropriate grief therapy. But whatever his rationale, I feel completely discounted. My eyes fill up as I move toward the closet to find the mandatory red dress.

*

"You look beautiful," Rob says as he helps me out of the car. I think he means it, but I feel anything but fetching right now. Concealer applied with a trowel and multiple squirts of eye drops can only do so much.

"*One* family lives here?" I say as we walk toward what looks like a resort hotel. The front courtyard is dotted with sculptures, and the immaculately groomed trees are lit with what seems like a million tiny, flickering white lights. I remember Mom used to say that she hated tree lights that blinked on and off because they gave her a headache. I smile to myself, which Rob mistakes as renewed enthusiasm for the whole party plan.

"See? I knew you'd be glad you came. Just look at this place," he says, squeezing my hand. "I could definitely get used to this."

"We could fit our house in here six times over," I say. "Good thing Phoebe is microchipped. We'd need it to find her if she ever left the bedroom."

Rob starts to answer, but then his gaze shifts over my shoulder. He breaks into a giant grin and starts walking, pulling me along with him.

"There's the big boss," Rob says, sounding a little like a kid who just saw Santa. "Let's go say hello."

The big boss in question is Davis Callerstrom, founder and CEO of Callerstrom Information Systems. According to Rob, they make the most popular molecular modeling software in the country. As a confirmed technophobe who failed basic chemistry, I am still unclear as to the intricacies of this ground-breaking product, much to Rob's chagrin. All I know is that it helps scientists to mimic the stuff that the molecule thingies do, so they can develop more new drugs and continue making the pharmaceutical industry very happy.

As we make our way through the crowd, Rob lets go of my hand, and I hurry to keep up with him. Just as we approach Davis and his wife, the heel of one of my sandals catches on a crack in the pavement. I stumble and nearly go ass over teakettle right in front of them.

"Are you okay?" Davis asks, reaching out to steady me.

"Oh, I'm fine," I say. "Just trying to break the world record for the cocktail party 100-yard dash. Should've gone with the Nikes instead of Jimmy Choo." He grins at me as his wife gives me a look of utter derision.

"Davis, Lydia, this is my wife, Charlotte," Rob says.

"Good to meet you, Charlotte," Davis says, giving my hand a firm shake. Lydia extends her hand toward me in a manner that suggests I should kiss it while genuflecting. I clasp her hand, and it's limp and cold.

"Well, it's really nice to meet you both," I say. They nod in acknowledgment, and Davis flags down a server with a giant tray of champagne flutes. We all reach for a glass, and Davis clears his throat before raising his in Rob's direction.

"Here's to Rob. A true rising star at CIS," Davis says, as they clink glasses. We all follow suit with our beverages, and I do my best to look proud instead of exhausted.

"Thank you, Davis," Rob says. "This company means everything to me. You know that."

"I do, indeed," Davis says before turning his attention to me. "I have big plans for your husband, you know."

I just nod and smile, hoping I don't look too Stepford. *God, I just want to go home.*

Rob shoots me a look, then leaps in to fill the void. "We can't wait to hear what you've got in store," he says, putting his arm around my shoulder.

"In due time," Davis says, giving me a wink as he tosses back the last of his champagne. "Mr. Grayson, what do you say we trade these in for a couple of *real* drinks?"

"Excellent idea," Rob says as they head off to the bar, leaving me with Lydia to prattle on about God knows what. I do a quick mental tally of socially bland topics, but Lydia beats me to the punch by making small talk about my job.

"So, do you… work?" she asks. The word *work* seems to get stuck in her mouth. Like she's trying to pronounce an expression she heard once in some foreign land.

"Yes, at a family law firm," I say. "Front office administration."

"Mm-hmm," Lydia nods, taking a sip of her champagne. "I was a secretary once, too. Before I had our children."

Secretary? I can't tell if she's being condescending, or if she honestly thinks that's the proper term for office staff in these here modern times.

"Do you have children, Charlotte?"

"No kids. Just our dog, Phoebe," I say, hating myself for sounding apologetic for not having procreated. "But Rob's side of the family has lots of nieces and nephews, so we're covered."

Lydia's face pinches up into some sort of hybrid of disdain and pity. "Well, that's nice. Children are life's greatest blessing."

I begin silently praying to the Cocktail Gods that Rob will show up with either a drink or a pregnant woman in tow so that Lydia will have someone to talk blessings with.

"Of course they are," I say. "But so is Phoebe. I couldn't love a child any more than I do her."

I know this is absolutely the wrong thing to say, but I can't help myself. I told Rob I wasn't in the mood for chatter, and this filter-free moment I'm having is exactly why. Still, I try to salvage things before the guys come back.

"So, how many kids do you have?" I ask, hoping I sound genuinely interested.

"Two boys and two girls," Lydia says, reaching for her phone. I commence with smiling and nodding as she flips through photo after photo of some admittedly good-looking young people.

"Our twin girls are seniors in high school this year, and our boys are both in college," Lydia says, beaming. "Actually, our oldest son is married. He and his wife are expecting their first child next month."

"Well, congratulations, Grandma!" I say. Lydia's face immediately darkens, and I realize that calling a woman whose face pays the mortgages of half the plastic surgeons in Los Angeles the G-word is a huge mistake.

Just as I begin the futile exercise of backpedaling, Rob and Davis appear with drinks in hand. Lydia glares at me and takes her husband by the arm.

"Let's go inside," she snips. "I'm sure Rob and Charlotte would like to socialize with some of the other guests."

"She's right," Davis says. "Don't want to monopolize you two all evening! Enjoy the party, and we'll catch up in a bit." Rob watches Lydia practically drag Davis through the crowd, before turning on me.

"What was *that* all about?"

"She asked if we had kids. And when I told her no, she acted like I was a lesser human being for having left my uterus vacant. So, I told her about Phoebe and said that I loved her as much as any child."

"That's it?" Rob says.

"And then I called her Grandma."

"You did *what*?" Rob looks like he's about to have a stroke.

"Her son's wife is due any second, and I congratulated her on her impending Grandma-hood. Apparently, she finds the word offensive."

"Seriously?" Rob exhales loudly and shakes his head. "Couldn't you have called her Nana or Gigi or something that doesn't make her sound like a crone?"

"Calm down. I'm sure she's already texted her cosmetic derm that she needs emergency Botox on Monday. She'll be fine."

I can tell Rob wants to say a lot more. But making a scene in front of everyone would likely put a damper on his budding corporate bromance with Davis.

"Just stick to the weather next time, okay?" Rob mutters. "If there *is* a next time, that is."

"I'm sorry. I told you my coming tonight was a bad idea…"

"And this was your way of proving you were right?" Rob says. "Thanks."

I start to defend myself but decide against it. He's already pissed, and anything I say is going to make things worse. Taking a page from the big boss, I just shrug and dutifully follow my spouse as he weaves his way through the crowd.

Chapter Seven

"It's almost five o'clock. You keep chugging that stuff, you won't sleep tonight," Will says as he watches me down yet another cup of crappy office coffee.

"I didn't get home from Rob's big corporate bash until almost one thirty this morning. Caffeine jitters are the least of my worries."

"What kind of idiot throws a huge party on a Sunday night?" Will says.

"The kind that owns the company."

"Ah, command performance?" Will asks.

"Pretty much," I say. "But it was important for him to impress the head honcho, so I took one for the team."

"You're a good soul."

"I don't know about that," I say, recalling the tension between Rob and me after the Grandmagate debacle.

"I know you're tired, but you seem… upset." Will says.

I don't answer him, reaching for my phone instead. I've texted Rob a few times today. Not about anything particularly important, just trying to make some sort of conciliatory contact. He hasn't responded.

"Char?"

"I'm fine," I say. "I just need to get out of here, go home and crash." I can feel him watching me as I gather up my things, avoiding his eyes as I dart toward the door.

*

After I start up the car, I find both myself and the engine idling. My foot still on the brake, I glance at my phone again, feeling the sting of resentment as I scroll through my unanswered texts. *Why am I trying so hard to make amends when I didn't do any-*

thing wrong? So, maybe I wasn't the perfect Corporate Wife-A-Tron. But it's not like I got drunk and dove into one of the multiple fountains at Chez Callerstrom. And even though Lydia thought I was the antichrist, Davis seemed to like me just fine.

But I'm actually more exhausted than angry right now. I'm tired of trying to mentally defend my position as the one in the right. Maybe I *was* selfish for not putting on a better show of wifely support. I don't know, and right now, I don't care. I dial Rob's number before I can change my mind. He picks up instantly.

"I know I haven't answered your texts. I've been slammed all day. What do you need?"

I'm so taken aback by his tone, I almost forget what I was going to say. "I just thought… maybe we could meet somewhere. I'm just leaving the office, and…"

"I can't," Rob says. I hear people chattering in the background, and I can tell he's trying to keep up with the conversation while half-listening to me. "I'll catch you later at home, okay?"

"Sure," I say. "What time do you think you'll be there?"

"No idea," Rob says. "Gotta go." He hangs up before I can respond.

I turn the car engine off and toss the phone onto the passenger seat. My chest tightens, and I blink back tears, furious that I'm allowing his brush-off to upset me this much.

After a moment, I hear someone tapping on my window. I turn to see Will peering at me through the glass, and I swipe quickly at my eyes before rolling down the window.

"I thought you were all fired up to get home and crash," he says.

"I was. I mean, I am."

"Then why have you been sitting out here for 10 minutes?" he asks.

"It hasn't been that long," I say. "What, am I on a shot clock?"

"No, smartass," Will says. "I just wanted to make sure you were all right."

He starts to walk away, but I put my hand on his arm. "I'm sorry. I'm just… it's hard to explain."

"Probably much easier to clarify over a glass of wine," he says.

I hesitate a beat too long, and he closes the deal.

"Meet me at Trask's."

*

"You look like you're casing the joint," Will says as we walk into Trask's. "What's up?"

"Nothing," I say. But he's right. My eyes are darting around the room to see if anyone from the firm is here. The fact that I'm even remotely concerned about someone seeing us together makes me question myself. "Let's go sit down."

Will and I take a seat at the end of the bar, and I ask for a glass of house chardonnay. I wait for Will to follow suit, but he's busy perusing the lineup of liquor
bottles on the wall behind the bar.

"I'll have a Jameson, neat," he says to the bartender.

"Going high octane this evening?" I say.

"I've always liked whiskey, but Shelly hates the stuff," Will says. "But I'm a
grown-ass man, and she's not here." As the bartender puts down our drinks, Will
grabs his glass and clinks it against mine.

"So, why were you sitting in the parking lot crying?" he asks.

"I wasn't *crying.*"

"Fine." Will shrugs and takes a sip of his drink.

"All right. So, Rob is pissed at me, and things are a little tense," I say. "I didn't
exactly hit it off with the CEO's wife at the party."

"What, did you throw a drink at her or something?"

I shake my head. "She told me one of her sons was about to become a father,
so I said, 'Congratulations, Grandma!' She didn't love it."

"*That* was your huge offense?" Will laughs, almost spitting out his drink.

"Yeah. I couldn't believe it was such a big deal," I say.

"To granny or to Rob?"

"Both. Well, mainly Rob," I reach for my wine and take a larger-than-intended
chug. "I know he was freaked out about making a good impression. But it was like
he thought I upset her on purpose."

"That's bullshit," Will says. "You didn't even want to go, but you did anyway to
support him."

"No good deed goes unpunished."

Will nods. "You just paraphrased my entire life."

I am starting to feel not only the wine but a nagging sense that I'm betraying
Rob in some way. I'm still upset with him, but I probably shouldn't be talking about
this stupid incident and making him look like a jerk. I start to change the subject,
but Will is locked on.

"I go through the same crap with Shelly all the time," Will says. "You try to do
something nice, and it backfires in spectacular fashion."

"Well, it's true that I didn't want to be there," I say. "And I probably gave off that
vibe. I'm sure that didn't help."

"So, now it's all *your* fault?"

"I'm a recovering Catholic," I say. "Guilt is like salt. I sprinkle it on everything, whether I need it or not."

"Don't worry. Father Will is here to absolve you," he says, flagging down the bartender and motioning for two more drinks. I'm not even halfway through my glass, but his apparently has a leak in it.

"Thanks, Padre," I say. "But to be fair, I haven't been the same since Mom died."

"No shit," he says. "You lost your mother. How the hell did he expect you to be the fucking life of the party?"

I shrug and dump what's left of my first glass of wine into the second. "I have no clue," I say. "About that, or much of anything else when it comes to him these days."

"It's like we talked about at lunch the other day," Will says. "The whole growing apart thing."

"*We* didn't talk about it," I say. "*You* did."

"I shouldn't presume," Will says. "But I felt like maybe you understood my situation a little more than you cared to admit."

"Perhaps," I say. "But there's more good than bad. I mean, you're not going to make it seventeen years without things changing."

"Agreed," Will says. "But shouldn't they be changing for the better?"

I nod, and Will continues. "I know Shelly and I got off to a rough start with the insta-family," Will says. "But she's a great mom. The boys are her world, and I've always appreciated that about her. But…" He falls silent, staring down at his drink.

"But what?"

"I thought at some point she'd feel like being a wife, too," Will says. "But every day that she made it clear she wasn't interested, it made it a little bit easier to disconnect. Just do my own thing. You know?"

"Yeah. Well, no," I say. "I don't think Rob and I are really disconnected. He's just a little fixated on work right now."

"Ya *think*?"

"Look, he's always been ambitious," I say. "And I admire that about him. But this giant obsession with impressing the bigwigs… that's a recent development. I felt like I was more of a corporate prop than a wife at that party."

"Shelly's on cloud nine as long as she's got the kids and my credit card. Rob's in nirvana when he's hanging with the honchos and climbing the ladder." Will puts down his drink and leans forward, elbows on the bar top. "So, where does that leave us?"

I shrug. "Guess there's something to be said for finding your place in life. They clearly have."

"And you haven't?" Will says.

"My place is fine," I say. "Just do my job and go home. Works for me." I feel my eyes start to burn. Damn that second glass of wine.

"Not sure I buy that," Will says.

"I don't care what you buy," I say. "So, I don't *love* my job. Is that a crime against humanity?"

"If it were, half the planet would be indicted," he says. "So, what is it that you *do* love?"

"Paid time off."

Will shakes his head. "You don't owe me an answer," he says. "But please don't bullshit yourself. It's unbecoming." He hands me a cocktail napkin and motions toward my eyes. I'm simultaneously touched and furious that he's so perceptive.

"All right, you got me," I say, holding my hands up. "I'm a writer. And not a very good or persistent one, at that. I even found a writer's group, but I haven't gone yet because I'm scared. Which is why I'm riding a desk at a law firm instead of writing a novel. You happy now?"

"No. I'm not," Will says, his eyes softening. "And I think it's awesome that you write. Why didn't you ever tell me?"

"What for?" I say. "It's not like I have anything published."

"That's not the point," Will says. "At least you've got it in you to create something. That's what really matters."

"Tell that to Denise," I say. "One day I was stupid enough to try working on one of my stories at the front desk, and she snuck up and caught me in the act. I think I'd have been less humiliated if she discovered me making photocopies of my ass."

Will laughs, but the levity has drained from his eyes. "What's going on in there?" I ask, reaching across to tap his forehead. "And don't say 'nothing.'"

"When Shelly and I met, I was in film school," he says.

"Seriously? That's amazing!" I say. "Did you want to make features?"

Will shakes his head. "I didn't think I was gonna give Spielberg a run for his money. But I loved shooting. The lighting, the composition… all of it," he says. "I would've been happy making commercials, corporate videos… even doing still photography. Anything that put me behind a camera."

"So, what happened?"

"I was starting to get freelance work, but it wasn't coming fast or steady enough for Shelly's liking, especially since we'd started a family," he says. "I'd taken accounting courses, and since I'm good with numbers, that's what she pushed for. So, here I am: Chief Bean Counter."

"Will you ever go back to it?" I say.

Will waves his hand, dismissing me. "That's a story for another time," he says. "We're talking about you right now."

"I don't have anything else to say."

"No," Will says. "You've got plenty to say. Which is why you're writing stories when you're supposed to be logging time sheets."

I try to answer, but my throat is locked and dry. "It's a tough thing to silence your soul," Will continues. "Believe me, I've tried."

I stay silent, but my unspoken reply hangs in the air.

So have I.

*

Will and I are walking across the parking lot toward our cars. It's almost eight o'clock, and I wonder for a second if Rob will be upset that I'm getting home so late. Then I remember he had no idea when he'd be there himself.

"Where did you park?" Will asks as we approach his sedan. When we arrived earlier, the lot was jammed with happy hour revelers, so we had to find what spaces we could.

"I'm over there," I say, pointing to a spot about three rows away.

"I'll walk with you," he says.

"No, that's okay. I'll be all right."

"It's dark, and I'm not letting you out of my sight until I know you're safe," Will insists.

As we stroll, I can't seem to shake the image of Will behind a camera instead of a calculator. Or Denise in front of an easel, dabbing away at a canvas. *Why are we all so far from where our hearts have tried to take us?*

"Thanks for the drinks," I say, digging through my purse for my keys as we come up on my car.

"My pleasure," he says. "It was nice to talk about… things. Non-work stuff."

I pull out my keychain and click the fob to unlock my car door. I toss my purse onto the passenger seat and turn back toward Will.

"We really shouldn't have stayed out this late. I hope Shelly isn't too upset," I say. Will moves closer to me. "Ask me how much I care."

But instead of allowing me to ask the rhetorical question, he decides to kiss me instead.

I have about a million things stampeding through my head, not the least of which is that for a guy who hasn't kissed his wife in eons, he's pretty damned good at it. But that thought is quickly replaced by the knowledge that this little scenario is going to make things horrifically awkward between us at work. And whatever issues Rob and I may have, they aren't going to be solved by me making out with my co-worker in a parking lot.

"I gotta go," I say, untangling myself from Will.

"I guess I should apologize to you for that," he says. "But I'm not going to."

"No need to. I mean, we both… never mind," I say. "But you know it was a bad idea, right?"

"I know of no such thing," he says, taking my face in his hands and planting a soft kiss on my forehead. "See you tomorrow."

As Will walks away, I get into my car and settle in for the drive home. Just like I did earlier in the parking lot at work, I sit there, hot tears welling in my eyes. But this time, I can't blame Rob's rejection for what's going on inside of me.

Or more to the point, what seems to be trying to get out.

Chapter Eight

By the time I hit the door, it's close to eight-thirty. The house is strangely quiet, except for the clicking of Phoebe's nails on the tile as she runs over to greet me.

"Hey, you! Where's your dad?" I ask, looking around the room. Rob's car is in the garage, so he's got to be here. But he normally has the television or music going. The silence is beginning to creep me out.

"Hon?" I call out, walking toward our bedroom. I can see Rob is already stripped down to his underwear and crawling into bed.

"Where were you?" he asks.

"Spur of the moment happy hour," I say. "You said you didn't know when you were going to be home, so I figured it'd be no big deal."

"It's not," he says. "Can you turn off the light?"

"Sure," I say. "But why are you going to bed so early?"

"I've got a six o'clock tee time in the morning," he says.

"On a weekday?"

"It's a team-building thing with my staff, okay?" Rob says. "Can you either come to bed or hit the light on your way out?"

I don't really want to go to bed right now. But I feel like going off to hang out on the couch by myself would just add one more degree of separation between us. So, I turn off the light, slip out of my clothes and get into bed. He's lying on his side, with his back facing me. I reach out to touch him, but he's already snoring softly. I pull my hand back and stare up at the ceiling fan, hoping its spinning blades will lull me to sleep.

*

It's only five o'clock in the morning, and it's barely light outside. But Rob is already up, dressed and gathering his golf gear. I hear his keys jangling in the kitchen, so I drag myself out of bed to catch him before he leaves.

"I thought your tee time wasn't until six?" I say, rubbing my eyes and stifling a yawn.

"It is, but I need to hit the driving range first," he says.

"At this ungodly hour, I doubt you'll have much company," I say.

Rob shrugs and starts rummaging in his golf bag. He seems distracted and tense, which isn't normal for him when he's about to play a round of his favorite sport. I grab a thermal mug, fill it with coffee and hand it to him.

"One for the road," I say.

"Thanks," he says, giving me a half-smile.

"Are you all right?" I ask. "You seem upset with me." *And if you knew what an idiot I was last night, you would be.*

"I'm sorry if I was short when you called yesterday," he says. "I'm under a ton of pressure. I can kick some ass at CIS, but I've got to prove myself to Callerstrom."

"I think you already have," I say. "He couldn't stop gushing about you at the party."

"Doesn't matter," Rob says. "He should have 'what have you done for me lately' tattooed on his forehead."

Rob hoists his bag over his shoulder and gives me a quick kiss. "Hey, remember it's your 45th this weekend," he says. "Let's go someplace nice to celebrate."

"I'd love that," I say. *We just need a little time to reconnect. Everything will be fine.*

As Rob flies out the door, I start thinking about my birthday. Not where we'll go for dinner or what he might give me as a gift. It's the number that's got my attention.

Forty-freaking-five. My life is half over… if I'm lucky.

I shake my head and berate myself out loud, hearing Mom's voice spring from my mouth. "Charlotte Elizabeth, knock it off. Enough drama. It's just a birthday."

I consider crawling back into bed for a while. But in spite of a lousy night of sleep, I'm not the least bit drowsy. So, I pour myself a cup of coffee instead and take Phoebe into the backyard so we can watch the sun come up.

"Your mom feels like a big jerk," I say to Phoebe, who responds by trotting off to pee on the grass.

I know that what happened with Will was a mistake. But I have to admit that it was nice to feel that kind of chemistry with someone again. I look down at my right hand and see Mom's ring sparkle as the first rays of daylight dance off of it. It

38

makes me think not only of her, but this Daniel guy that was kissing her in the photo. And after my moment last night, I feel like I'm beginning to understand a little more where she was coming from.

"Come on, girl," I call to Phoebe. "Let's go back inside."

I top off my coffee and go back to the bedroom to retrieve Mom's box of mementos. I've got a few hours before I need to be at the office, so I should be able to sort through quite a bit.

As I sit down on the floor and start removing things from the box, Phoebe moves in closer to assist me. A thick, red leather-bound journal that I've just pulled out catches her attention, and she scoops it up in her mouth.

"Hey! Drop it!" I command, only to be ignored as Phoebe grips the book tighter in her teeth, wagging her tail and playfully daring me to take it from her. After a lap or two around the bedroom, I emerge victorious with the journal, now beautifully embossed with canine fang prints.

I open up the journal at random and start reading. The first thing I come to is a passage that makes me feel like my chest is imploding. After I remind myself to breathe again, I read it aloud.

My girl is a writer. I love the little poems she gives me. Filled with childish sweetness, but there is talent there. I hope she never gives up on her words the way that I feel like I have. Well, except when I'm with Daniel. He makes me feel like I actually have something to say. A true gift. He makes me believe in myself for one beautiful moment. But then it's back to reality. Not just the fact of having to physically leave him. But dealing with all the things in life that take precedence over the words that want to come out. Eventually, I know they will give up on me and find someone else. Someone like Daniel, who will bring them to life.

I feel Phoebe licking my cheeks, and I realize that she's doing her best to mop up the tears that have started pouring down my face. I'd seen Mom jotting notes now and then, which she'd tuck away as soon as someone came into the room. But I never knew how deeply she wanted to be a writer. Or how much faith she had that I could be what she never believed she could.

I look at the clock, and I know I should be acting like I actually have a job to go to. But I can't tear myself away from the box. I delve back into it and come up with a worn manila envelope marked *Encanto & Associates Press*. I open the envelope and pull out a thick pile of old articles, all neatly cut from various publications.

"My God…" I whisper as I begin sorting through the news pieces. They aren't just about Encanto and its huge success in the literary world. They are all focused on one of their star authors in particular.

Daniel Jameson.

My stomach lurches and my pulse jackhammers behind my eyes. It's all coming together.

Will's drink of choice last night.

Jameson.

Just like the whiskey… just like the whiskey…

Mom's last words.

This was the Daniel in the kissing photo. A man she hadn't seen in decades, and he was the last thought in her mind as she passed.

My hands are shaking so badly I can hardly sift through the pile of articles. But I can't stop until I piece this whole thing together, or at least a good chunk of it. I scan the pages one by one until I see what I hoped that I wouldn't.

It's a front-page spread in the *Los Angeles Times* entertainment section, profiling Daniel and his family. He is smiling and sitting with his arm around an attractive, petite dark-haired woman, with three young boys flanking them on either side. The caption tells me that his wife's name is Claire, and their kids are Colin, Trevor and Alex, ages fifteen, twelve and ten respectively. I check the date of the article, and it was published in September 1982. Right around the time when the photo of him kissing Mom was taken.

I continue leafing through the stack of articles, hoping to find something more current about Daniel. But every piece is yellowed, brittle and decades old, plucked from the time when he and my mother fell in love.

I put the pile aside and dip back into the box. Underneath a few paperback novels, I find an issue of *Writer's Digest* with the headline "Where Are They Now?" splashed across the cover, along with photos of several well-known authors who had faded into obscurity. Down in the lower right corner, I see a familiar face.

I open up to the article and find Daniel among the profiles. Unlike the other authors, he doesn't have a photo of himself writing in his home office, or doing whatever it is that keeps him busy these days. I scan the copy and the reporter notes that the interview was done over the phone "at Mr. Jameson's request."

All right, so he's a private guy, I think. I continue reading and Daniel answers the standard questions with guarded grace:

Doing any traveling? "Yes, if you count daily trips to the coffee shop."

Writing? "Strictly for pleasure."

Any plans to publish again? "Refer to previous answer."

Instead of using this interview to tell people he's still a viable literary presence, Daniel seems intent on painting a picture of contented retirement. But as I read on, things take a turn that it's clear Daniel didn't expect. And neither did I.

There have been rumors that a life-threatening illness is to blame for your absence from the public eye. Your fans still care a great deal about you. Would you like to set the record straight?

The reporter writes that Daniel stays silent for a long time before replying, and he wonders for a moment if the interview is over. But Daniel finally speaks:

"We are all in the process of dying. I just happen to be in conversation with several doctors about it."

The reporter presses for more information, but Daniel refuses to comment any further about his condition. The article goes on a bit longer, but I've learned all I need to know: the man that held my mother's heart is going to die, and her secrets will go with him.

I look back at the date on the cover and see that the issue is about six months old. So, it came out about the time Mom was starting to steadily decline and hospice was on the horizon. I picture her reading this and wondering, in spite of her own condition, if Daniel was going to be all right. My chest clenches in frustration as I realize that he could be at death's door, or already gone by now.

"Goddamn it," I mutter, flinging the magazine away from me. As it skitters across the floor, a few index card-sized papers fly out of the pages. Some of them are just subscription inserts, but one is a snapshot. As I walk over to pick it up, it looks to be a photo of Mom and Daniel at some sort of cocktail party. But there is a third woman in the picture. And I know her very well. My breath catches in my throat as I reach for my cell phone.

"Jana, can I come over?" I say. "We need to talk. I know about Mom and Daniel."

*

"Come on in," Jana says, her voice quavering a little as she gives me a hug at the door. "Let's go sit on the patio. I made us some iced tea."

I follow Jana through the house and out to the backyard where she has a pitcher, chilled glasses and a little plate of cookies set out.

"Thanks for letting me barge in on you with such short notice," I say as Jana pours the tea.

"No, it's okay. I understand. I, um…" Jana trails off, waiting for me to take the lead in the conversation. I reach into my purse and pull out a few photos. Her face blanches when I hand her the one of her, Mom and Daniel.

"So, you knew about them," I say.

"My God, where did you get this?" Jana whispers.

"It was in the box you gave me. Along with this," I say, handing her the photo of Mom and Daniel locked in an embrace.

Jana reaches for her tea and takes a huge gulp, exhaling loudly after she swallows. I think she's wishing that she'd have opted for something stronger.

"I'm sorry you had to find out about this the way you did," Jana says. "I hope you don't think less of your mom because of it."

"Not at all," I say. "It explains a lot, actually. I knew she and Dad were having problems, but I had no idea that another man was part of the equation."

"I don't think your father ever knew for certain that she was having an affair," Jana says. "But he did know that his sweet, domestic little Beth really started coming into her own once she started at Encanto."

"And he didn't like it at all," I say.

"But Daniel certainly did," Jana says. "I think he fancied himself as a bit of a mentor to her."

"That's one way to put it," I say.

Jana laughs and shakes her head. "When she started talking about this amazing author she'd met, I just figured she was a little star struck," Jana says. "You know how your mom loved her books."

I nod, taking a sip of tea. "I knew she loved to read. But when I looked through her journals, she talked about wanting to write, too. Did she ever tell you that?"

"She mentioned it now and then," Jana says. "Said that Daniel was trying to encourage her to do it."

"So, how did they finally get together?" I ask.

"Daniel was becoming a bit of a big shot, and he said that he needed his own office at Encanto," Jana says. "And of course, he'd require his own dedicated assistant, too."

"Smooth."

"So, once Beth was working for him, it was all over but the crying," Jana sighs. "And trust me, there was plenty of that."

Jana reaches for the picture at the party and stares at it for a long moment. "Beth and I got into a huge fight the night this photo was taken."

"Why?" I ask.

"It was a big bash that Encanto threw to celebrate *Breaking the Wheelhouse*, Daniel's debut novel," Jana says. "Your father refused to go, so Beth took me as her date. She wanted to be there for Daniel."

"But wasn't his wife with him?"

"No," Jana shakes her head. "If she had been, your mom wouldn't have gotten close enough to him to have this picture taken. She wanted Daniel, but she wasn't about to make waves in his family life. God forbid, he should ever have been inconvenienced." I can see Jana's hands gripping her glass tighter.

"And that's what you fought about?" I ask.

"Yes. I couldn't stand to see Beth making all the sacrifices while Daniel just enjoyed her when he felt like it, then went home to his family. And I told her as much," Jana says. "She didn't speak to me for months."

"Wow, I can't believe she cut you off," I say. "Mom wasn't like that."

"She said that he was the love of her life," Jana says. "And if I didn't understand that, then I didn't belong in her world."

"So, what did you do?"

"I apologized," Jana says. "I still felt the way I did about Daniel, but I couldn't bear to lose her as a friend."

"So, she kept on seeing him," I say. "For how long?"

Jana shrugged. "After we mended fences, I stopped asking questions. Now and then she'd disappear to what she called 'our place.'"

"Santa Barbara?"

"I suspected as much. But Beth would never tell me exactly where," Jana says, chuckling. "I think she was afraid I'd drive up there and give him a piece of my mind."

"Sounds like it wouldn't have done a bit of good," I say.

"None at all," Jana says. "I tried to tell her not to leave your father. At least not until Daniel made some sort of move toward a divorce. But she believed him when he said that it was only a matter of time before he left his wife. So, she jumped ship first, thinking he'd follow."

I start to reply to Jana, but the words dissolve in my mouth. A mix of anger and sadness sweeps over me, but something bigger trumps both feelings: a searing determination that is settling in my bones.

"Your hands are shaking," Jana says. "Are you okay?"

"Not really," I say, putting down my glass of tea. "Mom saved an interview with Daniel that came out pretty recently. He wouldn't give specifics, but he's very ill. For all I know, he's already dead."

"She was still following him," Jana says softly.

I nod, swallowing hard. "I know this is a lot to take in," she says. "In a situation like this, sometimes ignorance is bliss."

"No, ignorance is bullshit," I say. "Mom died with secrets she never told me. I'm not letting Daniel do the same thing."

Jana looks concerned. "What are you thinking, Char?"

"That it's time Daniel and I met," I say. "I'm going to find him."

Chapter Nine

"There's something I've wanted to talk to you about," Rob says as we sit down at our table at Trask's. Those words usually never lead to anything remotely resembling a happy discussion, so I immediately tense up. And being back at the scene of the crime, so to speak, isn't exactly helping my anxiety level.

"Fire when ready," I say.

"First things first," he says, flagging down a server and asking for two glasses of house red. He then reaches into his pocket and pulls out a small box.

"What's that?"

He gives me a bemused look, which melts into a warm grin that I haven't seen in quite some time. "It's your birthday, remember?" he says. "Gifts are kind of standard practice."

I feel my shoulders finally drop and relax. *He's really trying.*

Rob watches me as I remove the ribbon and take the top off of the box. Inside is something delicate and glittery.

"Wow... a charm bracelet?" I say. "I haven't had one of these in forever."

"Exactly why you should have one now," Rob says. "Do you like it?"

I pull it out of the box and examine each of the tiny charms. They're pretty, but they don't make any sense to me. One is a tiny replica of Big Ben. Another is London Bridge. And a queen's crown.

"It's really beautiful, hon," I say. "But I don't get the theme."

"Well, I have some news that will help explain it," he says. "You're quite possibly looking at the new Vice President of International Marketing."

"Oh, my God!" I say. "I had no idea there was even a position open!"

"It's a newly created role. Rumor has it that I'm their number one choice," Rob says. "Callerstrom is finally ready to expand overseas. They want to set up shop in England."

"That sounds amazing," I say, trying to imagine Rob hobnobbing amongst the Brits. "And think of all the flyer miles you'll be racking up going back and forth from here to the U.K.!"

"Well, not as many as you think," Rob says. "They want someone on the ground out there full-time."

"Wow," I say, feeling my heart leap into my throat. Thankfully, the server shows up with our wine. I take a sip as Rob continues.

"It's not set in stone yet," Rob says. "I still have to go through their interview process. You know, make it fair."

"But essentially, the position is yours if you want it," I say, trying to keep my voice from shaking.

Rob nods. "Just think. Living in London," he says. "How cool would that be?"

"Well," I say. "I mean, it's…"

"What's the matter?" he says. "You're getting all weird."

"I think it's an incredible opportunity," I say. "But we're talking about moving over five thousand miles away overseas. That's a pretty big deal."

Rob shakes his head. "I should have known you'd freak out."

"I'm not freaking out," I say. "There's just a lot to consider. I mean, think of Phoebe. She'd probably have to be in quarantine for, what, a month or so? That'd never work."

Rob smacks his forehead with his palm. "You admit this is an incredible opportunity, but I should turn it down because of the *dog*?"

"She's not just *the dog*, and you know it," I say.

"This job could literally set us up for a lifetime," Rob says. "I'd be making more than twice the salary I am now. You wouldn't even have to work. And then there are bonuses, stock in the company, and a ton of other benefits."

"It's a big deal. I get it," I say. "Just give me a little time to digest this. Okay?"

"All right," Rob says. "Just stop worrying about the details. We'll get everything taken care of."

Rob gets up from his chair. "I've gotta hit the head," he says. "If the server comes back, just order me the salmon."

As he walks away toward the restroom, I take the bracelet out of the box. I roll the tiny crown between my fingers, realizing that what I'd hoped was a thoughtful gift was just an attempt to warm me up to the idea of moving to jolly old England.

I hear my phone chiming in my purse, and I pull it out. It's a text from Will. *Happy birthday, Char. Wish I was there to help you celebrate…*

*

"Here you go!" Trina chirps as she drops a file box overflowing with paperwork on my desk, damn near knocking over my coffee in the process.

"What's all this?"

"It's for the Doctor Love case," Trina says, grinning.

"Who?" I ask, before recalling her ridiculous crush on our client. "Oh, you mean Dr. *Lovell.*"

"Yes! I swear to God, he looks like he was separated at birth from John Stamos."

I ignore her and point to the box. "Please explain this monstrosity."

"It's the doctor's disclosure documents," Trina says. "They're a total disaster. Erica wants you to organize them so Denise can do the exhibit prep."

"Okay, I'll get on it," I say.

"Great! We need to get this to opposing counsel by end of day tomorrow, so please make it a priority," Trina says, giving the papers a quick pat before heading back to her office.

I stare at the mess in front of me, and the urge to procrastinate is overwhelming. I reach into the box, pull out a pile of documents and spread them all over my desk, so I look like I've at least started the project. All I hear is the low murmur of office machines and clicking keyboards, so I'm pretty sure everyone is buried enough in their own work to leave me alone for a bit.

I know I shouldn't be researching Daniel at work, but I haven't been able to concentrate on anything else since I found out about his illness. Every minute counts and I have no idea where he is. His presence in the media dropped sharply after his *Wheelhouse* glory days, and he doesn't have a website. Still, I can't help but believe he's got some fans left in spite of his Salinger-esque seclusion. I run a search for Daniel Jameson fan pages, hoping that at least some of his admirers from back in the day have made it their mission to keep track of him.

Nice work, groupies, I think, smiling to myself as several fan sites devoted to Daniel pop up. I click on one called "Jameson's Wheelhouse," and the homepage masthead has a nice picture of Daniel that looks to have been taken well after his heyday. Just like Mom, he's aged well. Still handsome, but with the requisite gray hair and less than supple skin that comes with later years. I have to admit they would've made a great looking older couple.

The sidebar on the page has a "Latest Happenings" link, which seems odd. If he isn't really writing anymore, what could possibly be happening? I shrug and click on it anyway. There's probably just some little fan gathering at a coffee house where people sit around drinking lattes and dissecting one of his books.

"Holy shit…" I whisper. There is going to be a fan gathering, all right. But there's going to be a very special guest in attendance.

Daniel.

I fly through the copy, which says Daniel will be at Quinn's Books this weekend for a book signing. It doesn't mention anything about a new piece of work coming out, so an event like this seems a bit strange. Still, I grab a sticky note and jot down the date and time, along with the address for Quinn's. It's been a while since I've been there, but I vaguely recall they were very much into promoting local authors. So, maybe Daniel is still living here in Southern California, which would sure make tracking him down a hell of a lot easier.

I look at the gigantic pile of papers, then at the clock. I set the desk phone to go to voicemail and grab my purse. The giant mound of disclosure can wait. Time for an early lunch and a little book shopping.

*

I walk into Quinn's and my heart starts to do the quickstep. *What the hell is wrong with you? Calm down. It's not like Daniel is going to come marching out from behind the bookshelves.*

"Can I help you?"

"Huh? I mean… sure…" I say, turning to see a rather scholarly looking older man. "Sorry, I'm just… I've had a crazy morning. I just need to chill out and find something good to read."

"Then you came to the right place," he says, smiling and extending his hand. "I'm Quinn."

"Nice to meet you," I say, shaking his hand. "I'm Charlotte."

"We're not exactly Amazon, but I think we've got a nice selection," Quinn says.

"I'm sure you do," I say. "Actually, I've heard that you carry a lot of local authors."

Quinn nods. "We've got a lot of promising new talent in this town that never gets a shot. And then there are the established writers who get brushed aside once their star has faded. I like to look out for each of them."

"That's really great," I say. "Would one of those writers happen to be Daniel Jameson?"

"Absolutely," Quinn smiles. "You're familiar with his work?"

"Not yet," I say. "I've heard of his book *Breaking the Wheelhouse*, and I'd like to get a copy. Do you have it in stock?"

"Yes, right over here," Quinn says as he leads me towards a display of Daniel's books. He hands me a copy along with a promotional flyer from a stack sitting on top of the table. "He's doing a signing here in the store this weekend. You should come by."

"I'd love to," I say, glancing at the flyer. "Does he have a new book coming out?"

"No, not really," Quinn says. "I think he's been working on some short stories. I'm trying to talk him into doing a reading from one of them while he's here."

"Just curious, but why is he doing a signing without a new book to promote?" I ask.

"Well, he's been out of the public eye for a long time. Too long, in my opinion," Quinn says. "To be honest, I pushed him to do it. Told him it was time to get back in the game. Especially because of his..." Quinn trails off, seeming to catch himself.

"His what?" I ask.

"Nothing," Quinn says. "I just think it's time people rediscovered Daniel Jameson."

"Sounds like you're his biggest fan," I say.

"Daniel and I go way back," Quinn says. "We met in our first year of college in a creative writing class."

"So, you're a writer, too?"

Quinn laughs. "Not exactly. I loved writing, but I wasn't very good," he says. "So, Daniel went on to write books, and I built a not-so-illustrious career selling them."

As Quinn walks me toward the register to ring up my purchase, I wonder what he was holding back about Daniel. I have a lot more questions, but I decide to keep them to myself for now. I have a feeling Quinn could be my strongest link to Daniel, and I can't risk making him suspicious.

*

I check the time on my cell and realize I've only got about half an hour before I have to be back at the firm. I'm not the least bit hungry, so I'm not going to waste precious time trying to grab a table somewhere for lunch. Instead, I walk next door to Cinnamon's Bakery for a cup of coffee.

I grab my drink and settle in with *Wheelhouse*. I feel nervous cracking it open, almost as if I'm meeting Daniel for the first time. But I open it anyway and start reading the blurb on the inside of the jacket:

What do you do when the life you want to love, is the one you want to leave?

I close the front cover and try to catch my breath. I tell myself that I don't have time for this. That I'm going to be late if I don't head back to the office right now. That I'll get back into it when I can actually concentrate.

But I keep on reading.

Ray Marshall has it all. A thriving career as one of the nation's most high profile financial gurus, a beautiful wife and kids, and wealth that affords him a lifestyle that is the envy of all his friends and colleagues. And for a long time that was more than enough.

But when Ray finds himself increasingly trapped by a life that he feels is no longer his own, he spirals into a deep depression. Fueled by a profound sense of guilt over his lack of gratitude for his privileged existence, Ray sets out on a journey to reclaim his soul. One that will lead him out of his comfortable yet confining wheelhouse, into the unknown… and into the arms of a love he never expected to find.

I sit there, feeling the words sink into my skin. *Into the arms of a love he never expected to find.*

"Hey, you!"

I look up, startled to see Abby standing there. I haven't seen her since Mom's funeral.

"It's so great to see you," I say, standing up and giving her a huge hug. "I'm so sorry I've been out of touch. How are you doing?"

"All right," Abby says. "But I've had the morning from hell at the salon. One of my clients shows up with some god-awful home coloring experiment gone wrong and expects me to fix it in time for some hot date she's got tonight. I'm like, 'Honey, how many times have I told you, *back away* from the bleach?' But does she listen? Oh, hell no."

"So, what'd you do?" I'm seriously in the mood for one of Abby's crazy stories, but all too cognizant that the lunch clock is still ticking away.

"I wanted to just shave her damn head and throw her out the door," Abby says. "But somehow I managed to get the green toned down without frying what was left of her hair."

"Well, it sounds like a bitch of a morning, but I'll still trade you gigs if you're up for it."

"Ha! Are you kidding me?" she laughs. "I'd last about six seconds with those stick-up-their-ass attorneys trying to order me around. And you know I love you, but your creativity is non-existent when it comes to hair. When was the last time you changed your color?"

"When MTV still played music videos," I say, admiring Abby's latest shade of brunette streaked with some sort of bright, coppery auburn.

"I rest my case," she says. "So, what are you reading?" she asks, pointing at *Wheelhouse.*

I start to answer in detail but realize there is no way I can explain the book and the real reason why I'm reading it in under two minutes.

"It's an author I recently discovered," I say. "I'm going to go to his book signing this weekend. It's at Quinn's," I say, pointing next door.

"Sounds like a party," Abby says. "How about you and I find time for lunch next week? I can move clients around, so you tell me what's up with your schedule and we'll make it happen."

"That'd be perfect," I say, giving her another hug before I take off.

As I drive back to work, I think of how long Abby and I have been friends. We met in college, both of us working toward degrees we weren't sure we wanted but were told we needed in order to make it in the world. I forged ahead and dutifully finished my four years, emerging with a diploma in hand. Abby quit just three credits short of a degree.

"Are you crazy?" I screamed. "That's like, what, one class? Why drop out now?"

"Because I don't want to spend one more day doing something I don't want to do," she said, as if it made perfect sense.

As I pull into the firm's parking lot, I realize that it did.

Chapter Ten

As I arrive at Quinn's, I'm excited about seeing Daniel, but still uneasy. Here I am, about to meet the man that my mother turned her life upside down for, but he won't think that I'm anything more than just another geeked-out fan. I'm starting to wonder if this is really such a great idea.

I look around the room, which is starting to get surprisingly full. I knew Daniel had his devotees, but for someone who hasn't published new material in ages, this is quite a turnout. The crowd is a real mixed bag: college students, people my age, and quite a few seniors. Most of the older folks are holding copies of Daniel's books that look to be from the original printing.

"I can't wait to see Daniel!" a woman in her mid-sixties whispers loudly to her friend. "I just loved him. He was so handsome back then!"

"I'm sure he still is," her friend says. "I had a bigger crush on him than you did!"

I know someone that's got you both beat, I think, scanning the room for any sign of Daniel, or Quinn, for that matter. He put so much effort into getting people to come, I figured he'd be working the room like crazy.

People are starting to commandeer the few folding chairs that are set up in neat rows, facing a podium. I remember Quinn saying he was going to ask Daniel to read some of his new short stories, so maybe this will be more than just a signing after all.

"Everyone, we have an announcement!" one of Quinn's clerks calls out. The crowd rumbles a bit in surprise, but then falls silent. Quinn then emerges from the back room of the store and takes the podium. He looks worried and exhausted.

"I'm extremely sorry to tell you this, especially since you were all so kind to come out in support of a great author, and my good friend, Daniel Jameson," Quinn says, his voice strained. "But Mr. Jameson is unfortunately feeling under the weather and won't be able to make the signing today."

The crowd gasps collectively, then breaks into loud, agitated chatter. Someone calls out, "Is he going to be okay? Will you reschedule?"

"I'm sure he'll be fine," Quinn says, clearing his throat. "I do hope to reschedule the signing. I'll keep you all posted via our website."

"What's wrong with him?" a guy behind me bellows right into my ear. Quinn pretends not to hear him as I turn and give him a dirty look. I, too, want to know what's going on with Daniel, but screaming like a rabid tabloid reporter isn't the way to coax an answer from the only person who knows anything.

"Again, I'm so sorry for the inconvenience," Quinn says. "Your patience is much appreciated by both me and Daniel."

I watch as he turns to head toward the back room. The clerk pats him on the shoulder, and I can swear I see Quinn taking a quick swipe at his eyes. As the room buzzes with hushed concerns and speculations, I weave my way through the crowd, making a beeline for Quinn. As I get closer, I can hear his conversation with the clerk. I hang back just enough to make sure I stay unnoticed.

"Where was he going?" the clerk asks.

"Santa Barbara. I told him he was too sick to make the trip," Quinn says. "But he wouldn't listen. Had to get to… what the hell was that place called? It was a stupid name… oh, yeah, The Delinquent Dolphin."

"I think I've heard of it," the clerk says. "It's been around a long time."

"Well, he hasn't been there in decades, but suddenly he's hell-bent on going?" Quinn says, shaking his head.

They shift their positions, so Quinn's back is to me entirely. I momentarily lose their conversation, so I move in closer, straining to hear more.

"So, how was he found?" the clerk asks.

"He pulled over on the highway and got out of the car. Was stumbling all over the place," Quinn says. "Someone saw him and called 911, thank God."

"Holy shit," the clerk says. "He could've gotten run over."

"I know, I know…" Quinn says, rubbing his eyes and falling silent.

"You all right?"

"I really thought he'd forgotten about that place… those times. That he'd finally let it go," Quinn says softly, talking more to himself than the clerk who looks confused. "Hell, I don't know. Maybe it's the meds doing the thinking for him."

That place… those times. What had he thought Daniel had forgotten?

*

As soon as I hit the door, I go straight to the bedroom with Phoebe in hot pursuit. As I pull Mom's box out of the closet, she wags her tail expectantly.

"Not this time, girl," I say, shooing her away from the box. "I've seen what you can do to a journal."

Before I remove the lid, I grab my phone and do a quick search for *The Delinquent Dolphin Santa Barbara*. It pops right up, and I begin to peruse their extremely basic site. Aside from a few pictures of the rooms and the resort grounds, and a small "click here for reservations" button, there isn't much to look at. Maybe it was quite the destination back in the eighties, but now it seems like a plain-faced stepchild to the more luxurious hotels in the area.

Why is Daniel so hell-bent on going there now, after all these years? Maybe Quinn was right. It was some crazy cocktail of old memories and new medication that made him jump in the car in his condition. But there's got to be more to it.

I open the box and pull out Mom's red leather journal. It's by far the biggest of her diaries, so there is still much of it I haven't read. But I am going to go through every page of it—and every other notebook—until I find out more about the Dolphin and the time Mom spent there with Daniel.

Phoebe settles in next to me as I begin weeding through the entries. Some chronicle her feelings and insights; others are just lines of prose trying to morph into poetry.

But then I come to a page that is markedly different from the others. Her normally beautiful, flowing cursive is jagged and peaked, as if written by a shaky hand. The ink is smeared in spots shaped like splattered tears. I don't even have to read the first word to know she was beside herself when she wrote this.

Daniel wasn't here… he was supposed to meet me at our place. I needed him so much. But not for the reason I thought I would. I want to write about what happened, but I can't. I won't. Because that would make it all real. I almost called Fran, but… no. She would say I deserved it. It's awful to have a sister you can't share anything with. I should talk to Jana, but maybe she'd feel the same way as Fran. I don't know what to think anymore. But Marnie was here, thank God. She always is… doesn't trust the place to anyone else. But she knows what happened. And she's the only one who ever will. Not even Daniel.

I put the journal aside and press the heels of my palms into my eyes. Phoebe gives me a concerned lick on the cheek as I try to stop my mind from whirring. *Who the hell is Marnie?* I knew a lot of Mom's friends, and that's one name I don't ever

54

recall hearing. Jana has never mentioned her, and she wasn't at the funeral or the reception. I look back at the entry again, and something leaps out at me.

Marnie was here… she always is… doesn't trust the place to anyone else.

I grab my phone again and pull up my previous search for The Delinquent Dolphin and add the name Marnie to it. One of the first results on the list is a business profile from a local newspaper. I click on it and begin reading.

Marnie Blume is the founder and owner of The Delinquent Dolphin, located in the picturesque northern edge of Santa Barbara. Established in 1982, the resort is famous for its beautiful setting and stunning views, and has long been a favorite of locals and tourists alike.

I ignore the rest of the article and focus instead on the photo of a smiling woman, standing proudly in front of her establishment. She looks to be about Mom's age, but unlike my mother, is short, brunette and softly rounded. She has a warm smile, and I can instinctively feel why Mom was drawn to her. And with Mom and Daniel's romance being established at the same time as the Dolphin, I can see even more clearly how the connection was made.

But I know there's more than just the innkeeper-customer relationship there. Mom entrusted her with a secret she never told anyone else. And I'm not going to rest until I know what it is.

*

"So, where are we going?" I ask Will as he drives past several of the local haunts we frequent for lunch.

"A new place," he says. "I think you'll like it."

We keep driving for another minute or so before he turns onto a residential street and pulls up to a small apartment building.

"Okay, this is definitely not the sandwich shop," I say. "What's going on?"

Will doesn't answer and just waves his hand for me to follow him. I hesitate for a second before walking after him up a short flight of stairs to the second floor. He pulls out his keys and unlocks the door. I poke my head in cautiously before stepping across the threshold.

"You asked me the other night if I was ever going back to shooting," Will says, gesturing around the room. The tiny space is filled with camera equipment, a couple of laptops, and finished works tacked to the walls. "And the answer is, I never really left it. Shelly doesn't want my, as she so lovingly calls it, 'photo crap' all over our house. So, I rent this place."

As I walk around the room looking at some of his photos, I have to admit I'm impressed. The majority of them are black and white, and the subjects are everything from cityscapes to people of all ages. There is a familiarity in their eyes, which tells me he has a way of drawing them in.

"These are really good," I say. "Do you sell your work?"

Will shakes his head. "I used to in the beginning," he says. "But like I said, there just wasn't enough money in it. Every now and then someone will want to buy something, but I don't pursue it."

"You could put up a website," I say. "Just post the photos you've got now so people could buy them. Or hire you to do a shoot. You could totally do this as a side business."

"I appreciate your enthusiasm," Will says, giving me a small smile. "But right now, it's gonna have to be a hobby. Cash is king in my world, these days."

"Well, at least you're still doing it," I say.

"I can't *not* do it," Will says. "When I try to give it up, I'm miserable. Even if it's just a mind game, I have to at least pretend that I'm more than a bean counting ATM."

"Oh, come on," I say. "You wouldn't be keeping up a studio if you thought you were just fooling yourself about how good you are."

Will shrugs, walks over to a tiny refrigerator and pulls out two sandwiches from a local deli, along with bottles of iced tea. "I did promise to feed you, not just give a gallery tour," he says, putting the food down on a small coffee table.

"Well, thank you for both lunch and the tour," I say, grabbing one of the sandwiches. "I can't believe Shelly doesn't let you have this stuff at home."

"She doesn't appreciate anything that doesn't generate a steady paycheck," Will says. "So, what does Rob think of your writing?"

"He hasn't seen much of it," I say. "I used to share it with him a long time ago, but then I just… stopped."

"Why?" Will asks.

"I don't know," I say. "It wasn't a conscious decision. I mean, when I'd show him things I wrote, he was nice enough. But I could tell he just didn't get it. Probably the same way I don't get software code and the intricacies of corporate climbing."

"Sounds like Rob and Shelly should have lunch sometime," Will says, taking a swig of his tea. "But let's make a pact. I won't give up shooting if you don't give up writing. Deal?" He puts his hand out, and I momentarily flash back to our parking lot kiss. I grab his hand and give it a firm shake.

"Deal."

"You know, you're gonna need a head shot for your book jacket one day," Will says. "I know a guy who works cheap."

I smile and nod, taking a bite of my sandwich. "I guess I'd better actually write the thing before I start thinking about glamour shots."

"Oh, man, those are awful," Will laughs. "Eighteen pounds of makeup and so much filter it looks like you're in a fog bank."

"Throw in a spiral perm, and you just described every photo I ever took in the 80s."

"I can't imagine it," Will says, grinning. "All that natural beauty and you decided to make yourself look like a refugee from Twisted Sister."

"Well, good to know I was hot enough to join a band of metal-head drag queens."

"You know that's not what I meant," Will says.

"Yeah, yeah…"

"Okay, I take it back," Will says. "Forget the whole natural beauty thing. You're hideous. Feel better now?"

"I think that may have been the most bizarre trajectory a compliment has ever taken."

"And whose fault is that?" Will says, his eyes softening.

"I think we better get back," I say. "Divorce wars wait for no one."

Will shrugs and nods. I'm feeling the same pull toward him as I did that night at Trask's, and I know he can tell. As he gathers up the remnants of lunch, I absently check my phone for nothing at all. The vibe between us isn't particularly tense, just resigned. We both know the subject of "us" is going to remain a game of whack-a-mole until it's either embraced completely or dismissed for good.

Chapter Eleven

"So, how was your day?" Rob asks, grabbing two wine glasses while I stir a pot of spaghetti sauce. Phoebe weaves in and out of my legs, imploring me to drop a morsel of people food for her to snack on while I cook.

"Same old, same old. Another day, another dissolution," I say, as Rob pours some cabernet and hands me a glass.

"Funny you say that," Rob says. "You remember Jeff and Lena, right?"

"Yeah, but it's been a while. Were they at Callerstrom's party?" Jeff is one of Rob's best friends at work, but I've only met his wife Lena a few times over the years.

"No, they skipped it," Rob says. "Jeff just told me they've been separated for the past two months."

"Wow," I say. "What happened?"

"He didn't say much, but it sounds like Lena is going through some midlife crisis," Rob says. "She's been going to all these retreats. Wants to quit her nursing job at the hospital and become a *tantric healer*… whatever the hell that is. And she's gone vegan. Weird shit like that."

"So, she wants to reinvent herself," I say, feeling almost like I want to defend this woman I barely know.

"She's been married to Jeff for twenty years, and they've got two kids," Rob says. "Now all of a sudden she needs to turn into some grass-eating swami?"

"Swamis are men."

"Whatever!" Rob says. "The point is, he liked her the way she was. Everything was fine, and she had to rock the boat."

"Maybe they'll work it out," I say.

"I don't know. I'm just glad it's not us," Rob says, clinking his glass against mine. We both take a sip, and he continues.

"So, it looks like they're sending me to London," he says. "Probably before the end of the month."

"What for? I thought nothing was set in stone," I say.

"We've already been through this," Rob says, trying to mask his irritation. "Callerstrom has basically said I'm their guy. Meeting some of their people on the ground out there is one of the last few steps in the process."

"Okay, I get it," I say, turning my focus to stirring the sauce as my appetite dwindles to nothing.

"Why don't you come with me on the trip?" Rob says. "London is an amazing city. We could explore it together."

"I don't have any paid time off left," I say. "I burned it all up when Mom died."

"They made you use PTO for bereavement leave?" Rob says. "Screw them. Just quit."

"I can't do that."

"Why not?" Rob says. "When I get this promotion, you'll be out of there, anyway."

"That's a great offer, but I think you should just go alone," I say. "It'll be easier to focus on business if I'm not there bugging you."

"All right. If you want to stay behind, that's fine," Rob says. "But while I'm gone, I really want you to do some thinking about this."

"As if I haven't been?" I say.

"What I'm asking is that you try to figure out what you're so damned scared of," Rob says. "You're acting like you're being banished to the gulag instead of moving to one of the most exciting cities in the world."

"I'm sorry," I say. "I wish I could explain where all this is coming from." *In a way you would understand, accept, and not hate me for.*

"Don't apologize. Just figure it out," Rob says. "We're running out of time."

*

"So, how are things with you and… what was his name again?" I ask. "I'm sorry I haven't asked about him lately, but you'd just started seeing each other when Mom passed away." I can never keep track of Abby's constantly rotating cast of suitors.

"Andreas. The tennis pro," she says. "But it's over anyway, so you can forget his existence."

"What happened?"

"It's so stupidly cliché I don't even want to tell you," she says.

"He was sleeping with all his rich, bored housewife clients?" I say.

Abby nods. "Classy, huh?"

"Ugh. I really wanted to be wrong about that one," I say. "Are you doing okay?"

"Yeah, I'm fine," she says. "He was a jackass, anyway."

"The last thing you need is some middle-aged racquet club gigolo."

"True story," Abby says. "But honestly, I'm getting tired of the whole game, you know?"

"I hear you," I say. "But the right guy will come along at the right time."

"Careful, Hallmark will sue you for plagiarism," Abby says.

"Okay, I deserved that one," I say.

"I'm just giving you shit," Abby says. "I'm glad you found your Mr. Perfect early in the game, but I confess I'm a little envious. How's he doing, anyway?"

"Rob's fine," I say. "If there's anything 'perfect' about him, it's his obsession with his job. He's got that down to a science."

"Yeah, but he's doing really well, right?" Abby says. "I'd kill to date someone with a work ethic."

"Don't get me wrong, I admire that about him," I say. "It's just been tough since Mom's been gone. Maybe I'm expecting too much from him, but I feel like we're… orbiting around each other these days."

"Honey, you're still grieving," Abby says. "Nothing is going to feel right. Your job, your home life… maybe even your marriage. Everything is going to be off-kilter for a while."

"You're probably right," I say. "It's just a weird time right now for us, I guess."

"Well, forgive me for playing armchair shrink," Abby says. "But have you been writing? I think it'd help."

"Yeah, I know. I just…"

"You don't have to explain," Abby says. "But doing something you love instead of just knocking your brains out at the office will make you feel a hell of a lot better."

"You're right," I say. "I'll get on it, doc."

"Excellent," Abby says, clearly pleased with herself. "And who knows? The next book signing you go to may be your own."

"Oh, yeah. The signing," I say. "I did go last weekend, but the author was a no-show."

"Ah, bummer," Abby says.

I hesitate for a moment before continuing. "Well, it's a little more than a bummer," I say. "There was a reason I wanted to see him, and it wasn't just to sign my book."

I reach into my tote bag and pull out Mom's red leather journal with the photo of Mom and Daniel kissing pressed between the pages. I pull out the photo and slide it across the table to Abby.

"Oh, my God. That's Beth!" Abby says. "And who's that guy?"

"His name is Daniel Jameson. He's the author whose signing I went to," I say. "And he had an affair with Mom."

"No freaking way!" Abby shrieks, loudly enough for several people to turn and stare at us.

"My parents were still married when this shot was taken," I say.

I proceed to tell her all about the box Mom left behind, and the contents that have turned my life inside out. The more I talk, the further Abby's jaw drops.

"This is unreal," Abby says. "Did your Dad know about what was going on?"

"I don't know," I say. "But there was an inn in Santa Barbara that Mom and Daniel would go to. Look at what's written on the back."

Abby flips the photo over. "That's what she means by 'our place'?" Abby asks.

"Yep. I did some digging, and it's called The Delinquent Dolphin," I say. "It's been around since the time Mom and Daniel's affair started. And it's run by a woman named Marnie Blume, who apparently became really close to Mom."

"What makes you think that?" Abby asks.

"Mom wrote something in her journal that mentions her," I say, grabbing the journal and opening to the passage about Marnie that I read after rushing home from Quinn's last weekend. I start reading and look over at Abby when I'm done. Her face is pale and her eyes wide.

"What do you think the secret is?" she asks. "God, I hope it's nothing horrible."

"Me, too," I say. "But Marnie is the only one who knows the truth, and I've got to find out what it is."

"What are you gonna do?" Abby asks.

"I'm going to the Dolphin," I say, realizing that I just decided on it at that moment. "I want to see her in person. See the place where Mom lived a whole other life I never knew about."

"I'll go with you!" Abby says. "Sorry, you probably want to take Rob."

I shake my head. "I actually haven't told Rob anything about Mom's affair," I say.

"Why not?" Abby says. "I mean, he loved your mom, too. Are you worried he'd judge her?"

I start to reply but find myself shrugging instead in lieu of an answer. "I'll tell him sometime," I say. "But even if he knew, he'd never go with me. He'd think I was insane for tracking down a total stranger."

"Well, I could use a good adventure, so count me in!" Abby says.

"Rob's got a business trip coming up," I say. "He'll be gone for about a week. I'll leave Phoebe with Jana, and we can go then."

Abby beams and starts rattling off a ton of other things we can do when we're in Santa Barbara. But my mind is on one thing only: the secret only Marnie knows, and whether she'll tell me what it is.

*

I'm back at Quinn's today for the first time since the aborted book signing. I try to tell myself to take Daniel's no-show as a divine sign that I need to stop with all this amateur detective nonsense. And now with Rob campaigning for us to move to London, I've got plenty else to be thinking about. But no matter how much I try to distract myself from the incessant desire to meet Daniel face to face, it won't let up. So, here I am, wandering the aisles and pretending to shop while I plot my next move.

"Can I help you?"

I turn around to see Quinn standing there. "Yes, I've, ah, been reading *Wheelhouse*, and I think it's fantastic," I say. "I'd like to get some of his other books."

"Sure, they're right over here," Quinn says as he begins walking toward a display in the back of the store. "You've been in here before. Charlotte, right?"

"Yep, that's me," I say. "I've been in a few times. Last time was for Mr. Jameson's signing."

"Sorry about that," Quinn says.

"No worries," I say. "How is he doing? You'd said he was under the weather."

"I know what I said," Quinn says. "And he's fine."

"That's great to hear," I say. "I was just—"

"You said you were interested in some of his other works," Quinn says, handing me a book he seems to grab randomly off the shelf. "Try this one. It was the follow-up to *Wheelhouse*. Not as popular, but just as good, in my opinion."

"Thank you. I'm sure I'll enjoy it," I say, taking the book. "So, now that he's on the mend, any chance you'll reschedule the signing?"

"All right, what's up with the Spanish Inquisition?" Quinn says. I can tell he's agitated, but he's my only link to Daniel and the time for treading lightly is over.

62

"Look, I'm sorry if I seem pushy," I say, trying hard to appear contrite instead of desperate. "But I'm interested in more than getting him to sign my book."

"You don't say?" Quinn says, crossing his arms.

"I'm a freelance journalist," I say, the words spurting out before I can stop them. "I think Daniel... er... Mr. Jameson is brilliant, and I want to write an article about him."

"For what publication?" Quinn asks, still wary.

"Like I said, I'm freelance," I say. "Sometimes I work on assignment, but this would be on spec. Write it first, then shop it."

"And who would you shop it to?"

"Mostly online magazines that target younger audiences. Mainly, college students," I say. "I really feel like the up-and-coming generations need to know about him and his work."

Quinn relaxes slightly. "Well, I can't say I disagree with you, he says. "He does need a new audience."

"Absolutely," I say. "Once they discover how great his books are, I'm sure they'll be clamoring for him to write something new."

"Tell you what," Quinn says, reaching into his pocket for his cell. "Give me your number. I'll talk to Daniel about your idea for the article, and I'll let you know if he's interested."

"That would be wonderful," I say, before firing off my number. "Thank you so much!"

"Don't get too excited," Quinn says, motioning for me to follow him to the register to ring up my book. "You never know which way the wind's gonna blow when it comes to Daniel. But I'll put in a good word. That's all I can do."

Chapter Twelve

"I really wish you were coming with me to London," Rob says, throwing a few extra shirts into his suitcase.

I just nod and continue sipping my coffee as Phoebe leaps onto the bed to inspect Rob's packing job. He shoos her away from the suitcase and snaps it shut.

"I know how freaked out you are about moving so far away," he says. "And I'm trying to be patient and give you time to do some thinking."

"And I have been," I say.

"I know," he says. "But the process is moving along, and it's not going to be much longer before I have to formally accept the position."

"What would happen if you didn't?"

"You're asking me this *now*?" Rob says. "If you'd already decided you wouldn't move no matter what, why didn't you say something before I got this far?"

"I didn't decide anything," I say. "It was just a hypothetical question."

"It didn't sound like one," Rob says.

"Please just forget it," I say. "Look, if you've got the time, why don't you go ahead and scout things out while you're there. Condos, or whatever they call them. Flats?"

"Yes, flats," he says, a small smile forming.

"I want you to be happy," I say. "And I'm sure everything will be fine. In fact, it could be… quite the adventure."

Rob grabs my face between his hands and plants a kiss on my lips. "I'll email you info on the properties I check out, and we can talk about them when I get back."

"Sounds good," I say.

"Who knows?" Rob says, "We could be spending our eighteenth anniversary in London." He gives me a grin as he grabs his suitcase and dashes out of the bedroom.

I wait until I hear his car start up, then pull away from the house before I let the tears come. But I don't have the luxury of a meltdown right now. I've got to get ready for Santa Barbara and get Phoebe over to Jana's.

As I grab a small suitcase and begin gathering clothes under Phoebe's watchful eye, I start thinking about my question to Rob. I knew he was going to be upset with me, so why did I choose to bring up the possibility of him turning down the job? And more to the point, why am I not seeing this the way I should? A chance to start over in a new and exciting city with my husband. Traveling all over Europe. Having more than enough money so that I can devote myself to writing all day, every day.

But I can't shake the thought that this dream life Rob is proposing is conjuring up more thoughts of isolation than it is adventure.

*

As I arrive at Jana's, Phoebe is so excited she beats me to the front door. Jana opens it up before I can knock and Phoebe jumps up, gives her a kiss and immediately dashes inside.

"I'm going to miss you, too," I say, watching her explore the place like I'm not even there.

"No loyalty," Jana grins. "But I'm glad she's so comfortable here. You know I love her."

"That, I do," I say. "Thanks again for taking her on such short notice."

"So, where are you headed?" Jana asks.

"Just up the coast," I say. "Rob's out of town for business, and Abby and I haven't had much girl time in a while."

"So, you're just driving, and you'll see where you feel like stopping?" Jana asks.

"Yeah, I think so," I say. "Not really sure."

Jana pauses for a moment, giving me a look like Mom used to when she didn't believe a word I was saying. "You're going to Santa Barbara, aren't you? To look for Beth and Daniel's place."

I nod. "Actually, I've already found it," I say. "It's called The Delinquent Dolphin."

"Really?" Jana says. "I've never heard of it. How did you find out that's where they went?"

"Eavesdropping and the internet," I say, recalling Quinn's conversation with the clerk that sent me racing home after the signing.

"I can understand you wanting to know about the place they spent time," Jana says. "But why do you need to go up there?"

I glance back at the car which is still running. I planned on a quick drive-by to drop off Phoebe, but Jana isn't going to let me go without some sort of explanation.

"Come on," I say, motioning for her to follow me. "Let me show you something."

We walk back to the car, and I reach into my tote bag and pull out Mom's red journal. Jana leans against the car as I read her the passage where Mom wrote about the unnamed secret that she and Marnie shared. When I look up from the page, there are tears in Jana's eyes.

"Do you have any idea what she might be talking about?" I ask.

"No," Jana says, shaking her head. "I'd never heard her mention anyone named Marnie. And whatever happened, it doesn't sound like it was good."

"I agree," I say. "And that's why I have to see her in person. I've got to know the truth."

Jana dabs at her eyes. "Beth and I had our differences around that time. But I would have never, ever said she 'deserved' something—anything—bad to happen to her," Jana says. "That longing heart of hers made her suffer enough all on its own."

*

Abby and I are driving down the highway toward Santa Barbara when my cell rings. I don't recognize the number displayed on my dashboard, but I hit the button to accept the call. It goes to speaker, and Abby leans in, as curious as I am to know who this is.

"Hello?"

"Hi, Charlotte. It's Quinn." His voice sounds strained, "I wanted to get back to you about Daniel."

"Great!" I say. "How's he doing?"

"He's in the hospital," Quinn says. "Went in a few days ago. He'll probably be back home tomorrow."

"Oh, my God," I say. "What happened?"

"I don't want to speak out of turn," Quinn says. "I'll let him give you the details if he wants to."

"Fair enough," I say. "But you had a chance to talk to him about me?"

"Yes, I did," Quinn says. "He was flattered by your interest."

"Well, it's sincere," I say. "Did he say we could meet?"

"No," Quinn says. "But he didn't rule it out. I gave him your number."

"Do you think he'll call?" I ask, realizing that I'm starting to sound desperate.

"If he's feeling up to it," Quinn says. "No promises. I'm sure you can understand."

"Of course," I say. "I really do hope he feels better soon."

"Me, too," Quinn says, his voice breaking slightly.

"Thanks for letting me know what's going on," I say.

"Not a problem," Quinn says. "Good luck."

As Quinn hangs up, Abby wastes no time on the cross-examination. "So, this Daniel guy is really sick? What if he won't see you?"

"I don't know," I say, feeling utterly deflated. Granted, Quinn barely knows me, but I wish he'd been willing to offer up more specifics regarding Daniel's condition. And, selfishly, whether or not he thinks we have a shot at connecting. But if Daniel isn't doing well, probably the last thing he's thinking of is opening up his life to a stranger. Unfortunately, that's all I can think about him doing right now.

Chapter Thirteen

"Wow… this is gorgeous!" Abby says as we walk across the beautifully manicured grounds toward the lobby of the Dolphin. "No wonder your mom loved to come up here."

"Something tells me it was more about the company than the scenery," I say. But Abby is right. The place is lovely. The Dolphin is dwarfed by the multitudes of luxury resorts surrounding it, and it feels more like someone's home than a hotel.

When we enter the lobby, there is no one at the front desk. I wander along the walls, looking at framed autographed photos of some of their more famous guests. I don't see Daniel in the mix, but it's not a surprise. Publicity was the last thing he was seeking when he was here.

"Is that her?" Abby whispers.

As I look across the room, the same woman I saw in the website photo emerges from a back office. She sees the two of us, giving us a warm smile as she approaches.

"Welcome to the Dolphin," Marnie says. "How can I help you?"

I start to say something about how we just want to take a look around, we've heard so much about this place and other assorted touristy comments. But the words are lodged somewhere deep in my solar plexus, and my mouth has stopped working entirely. I can feel Abby staring at me as I continue to stand there mute.

"Are you all right?" Marnie asks. "Can I get you some water?"

"Yes, that'd be great," Abby says. "I think she just got really dehydrated on the drive up."

As Marnie walks away, Abby turns to me. "What's wrong with you?" she says. "You're acting like she's a freaking poltergeist or something."

"This was a horrible idea," I say. "Let's just leave."

"No way," Abby says. "Three seconds after we get in the car you'll be pissed at yourself, and I'll have to listen to you whine all the way back home."

I start to protest, but Marnie is walking up with two glasses of ice water with razor-thin lemon slices floating in each of them. She hands them to us, and motions toward a comfy-looking couch in a far corner.

"Why don't we sit down?" she says. Abby and I follow her and take a seat. "So, let's start over. What can I do for you?"

"You can talk to me about my mother," I say, watching Marnie's face cloud with confusion. "I'm Beth Reade's daughter. My name is Charlotte… and… I'm sorry… I shouldn't have just shown up, but…" Abby is already fishing for the tissues in her purse as the tears squeeze out of my eyes.

Marnie takes a deep breath, and I can see her trying to steady her own emotions. "I haven't seen Beth in ages," she says. "But we were very close once."

"I know. And that's one of the reasons I'm here," I say. "Mom passed away recently."

"Oh, my God," Marnie says, her eyes welling up. "What happened?"

"Cancer," I say. "But I was with her at the end, and it was peaceful. I'm grateful for that."

Marnie nods, swallowing hard. "So, how did you find me?" she asks. "And I suppose, more to the point, *why*?"

"When Mom died, she left me a box full of photos and journals," I say. "And most of what she wrote about was a man she loved named Daniel Jameson." I pull the photo of Mom kissing Daniel out of my purse and hand it to Marnie. She stares at it for a long moment.

"I was the one who took this picture," she says. "Everyone knew them as a couple around here. They were inseparable."

"And I never knew a thing about him until she was gone," I say. "So, I've been trying to track him down."

"Any luck?" Marnie says.

"Yes and no," I say. "I know he's still living in Southern California, but he's in very bad health. In fact, I've been told he's in the hospital."

"What's wrong with him?" Marnie asks.

"I don't know the details," I say. "But I'm pretty sure it's something serious. He may not have much time left."

Marnie falls silent, and I can see her wheels turning. "I hope you had plans to stay here tonight," she says.

"We've actually got reservations someplace else," I say.

"Nonsense," Marnie says. "You're staying with me. My treat."

"You really don't have to do that," I say. "I'm sure you've got a full house, and—"

"You know what? I'm starving," Marnie says, ignoring my protest. "Let's get you to your room. We'll have an early dinner and a nice long chat."

"I'll go grab our bags from the car," Abby says.

"This is really kind of you, Marnie," I say. "Thanks."

"Well, you've come this far," she says. "And what I have to tell you isn't a one-cup-of-coffee kind of conversation."

*

As soon as we sit down at our table, Marnie motions to a server who appears with a carafe of wine and three glasses.

"I like the way you think!" Abby says to Marnie, as the server begins pouring. Marnie smiles as she reaches for her glass, raising it to the two of us.

"To new friends," she says. "And old stories."

After we all clink glasses and take a sip, I reach for the red journal in my tote bag. "I want to read you something Mom wrote," I say. "It's what made me realize I had to come here."

I open the journal and read the passage where Mom talks about the secret that only Marnie knew. By the time I'm done, Marnie is in tears.

"Even if it was something she wouldn't tell him, why wouldn't she at least write about it?" I say. "God knows, she recorded everything else that was going on in her life with Daniel."

Marnie wipes her eyes and takes a deep breath. "Your mom and Daniel used to come up here all the time. Right after they got together, and for a few years after that. He'd go hole up in their room to work on his latest project, and Beth would come have coffee with me, or just walk around the grounds. Sometimes I'd see her sitting by the pool, writing in the journal you just showed me."

"Okay, so what about the secret?" Abby interjects.

"Jeez, Abby," I say. "Let Marnie finish."

"It's okay. You came for answers," Marnie says. "And this one won't be easy to hear."

"Nothing has been easy since she died," I say. "Just tell me."

Marnie takes my hand. "Charlotte, your mother had a miscarriage," she says. "It was Daniel's baby."

Abby lets out a shriek, but I can't even breathe. "What... how did it happen?" I whisper.

"They'd arranged to meet up here for the weekend like they usually did. But he cancelled at the last minute," Marnie says. "Beth was crushed. She was so excited to tell him she was pregnant."

"But, he was still married," I say. "How did she think he was going to explain a baby to his wife?"

"She thought maybe he was finally ready to leave her," Marnie says. "She saw the baby as a sign. She said she had a hard time conceiving you, and it was a miracle that she was pregnant again."

"So, why did he cancel?" Abby says.

"He was up for a National Book Award for *Wheelhouse*," Marnie says. "The ceremony was in New York, and he had planned to skip it. He was happy about the honor, but public appearances weren't his thing. He could be a bit reclusive."

"I believe it," I say, thinking of Quinn's remarks about struggling to convince Daniel to get back in front of people.

"But all of a sudden, it was imperative that he be there," Marnie says. "Said something about his management insisting he go. I never saw him as a man who would take orders from anyone, so it seemed odd to me that he caved in. Especially when he'd have to be there without the person who made the book possible."

"What do you mean?" I say.

"He wrote *Wheelhouse* during his early days with Beth. It was for her," Marnie says. "It was *about* her. How she made him feel like his true self when they were together."

"So, what did Mom do when he told her he wasn't coming?" I say.

"She put on a brave face. Told herself they'd see each other soon after the awards," Marnie says. "But when he backed out of their weekend, she knew something had shifted between them. She could feel it. The next night, she miscarried."

"But why didn't she ever tell him?" I say.

"Beth wanted his love, not his pity," Marnie says. "And when he pulled away, she just shut down. Didn't beg or pursue him. And of course, she left Encanto right away."

"I remember when she told me she quit," I say. "I was shocked because she loved that job. But when I asked her why she left, she just brushed it off as 'the industry was changing.'"

"That's one way to put it," Marnie says, shaking her head. "She felt that Daniel had simply gotten too big for her. But I didn't buy that. There was something else going on that was more than an overblown ego. I just knew it."

"Holy shit, *more* secrets?" Abby says.

"I believe so. But I could never uncover them," Marnie says. "Beth would have killed me if she'd known this, but I tried reaching Daniel through his publisher. Got stonewalled at every turn."

"So, that was it?" I say. "He just disappeared?"

Marnie nodded. "And so did your Mom," she says. "That weekend was the last time I ever saw her."

Chapter Fourteen

"So, how was your weekend?" Will says, leaning against my desk.

You have no freaking idea. "Pretty nice. Rob's out of town, so I went up to Santa Barbara with a girlfriend of mine," I say. "How was yours?"

"Definitely not a cruise to the beach," Will says. "I slept in my studio Saturday night, after Shelly and I had a blowout."

"I didn't think you had those leave-the-house kind of fights," I say.

"We usually don't," he says. "When things get bad, we just ignore each other. But this time she pushed too far."

"What do you mean?" I say.

"Ever since her best friend's husband went back to school for his MBA, Shelly has been hinting that I should do the same," Will says. "At first the nudges were subtle. Telling me how much he loved his classes. Leaving a university brochure on the kitchen counter."

"Annoying, but tolerable," I say.

"Yep. And when he graduated last month, I thought maybe the topic would finally be off her radar," Will says. "But she just found out that he got recruited away from his firm at twice the salary he was making before. So, now she's cranked to eleven to get me back in school."

"And you said no way in hell," I say.

He nods. "I tried to be nice. Told her that I was just too overloaded at the office to pile coursework on top of everything," Will says. "But she just blew right past that and started in with how it would only be for a few years, and she knew I could handle it."

"Says the full-time soccer game chauffeur."

"Exactly. And I did take the liberty of pointing out that she attends way more girls' lunches than she does games," he says. "That's when she came unglued. Told me I have no idea how hard she works raising the boys. That they are going to be in college before we know it, and I owe it to them to have money set aside for tuition and anything else they need."

"So, she went for the guilt," I say.

"Yeah. But when that didn't work, she switched to dictator mode," he says. "Told me—and I quote—'Stop fucking around with photography and work on something that actually has a prayer of making money.' That's when I split." Will's voice is controlled, but his eyes reflect something I haven't seen in him before: sheer defiance. And I have to admit, I feel proud of him for standing up for his passion in the face of the Suburban Paycheck Police.

I'm about to launch into a tirade that I will probably regret when my cell phone rings inside of my purse. I grab it and notice that the incoming number is marked as private. Normally, I wouldn't pick up, but something tells me I should.

"So sorry, but I gotta take this," I say.

"No worries," Will says. "I'm done venting."

"I seriously doubt that," I say. "We'll finish later, okay?"

Will nods and walks away. I manage to answer just before the call goes to voicemail. "Hello?"

"Is this Charlotte?" an unfamiliar male voice asks.

"Yes," I say. "And who am I speaking to?"

"My name is Daniel Jameson. I understand you might be interested in interviewing me for an article you're writing."

"Oh, my God," I blurt. "I mean, yes. Absolutely. I would love to."

"Wonderful!" Daniel says. "Would you like to do it by phone, or in person?" I'm surprised by his enthusiasm but grateful for it, especially in light of his reticence during the last interview I read.

"In person would be great," I say, trying to keep my voice from shaking. "What's your availability?"

"Well, being all but put out to pasture by the literary world, I'd say I'm pretty open," Daniel says. I can hear a smile in his voice.

"I hate to impose on your weekends or evenings," I say. "But I have a day job right now, so would either of those be possible?"

"Take your pick," Daniel says.

"How about this weekend?" I ask. "Sometime on Saturday morning?"

"I'm an early riser, so why don't we chat over coffee?" Daniel says. "Do you know Cinnamon's?"

"I do," I say. "It's my favorite coffee joint."

"Then let's meet there at nine," Daniel says.

"Perfect!" I say. "And thank you so much for allowing me to interview you. I'm truly honored."

"No, *I'm* honored," Daniel says, his voice slightly wistful.

"See you Saturday," I say, my chest hammering as a sobering reality washes over me. In just a few days, I'll be face to face with the world-famous author who captivated my mother's heart.

*

I walk into Cinnamon's and look around for Daniel. It's not very crowded, but I don't see him anywhere. I start to get nervous, wondering if maybe he's changed his mind or isn't feeling well again. I take a seat near the window so I can watch for him while I review my notes. Aside from poring over Mom's assorted notebooks, I did some background research on the less personal aspects of his life and found out that he was a journalism major in college. My stomach starts doing flips as I consider that there is an excellent chance I will embarrass myself by trying to impersonate a real reporter.

"Mr. J., good to see you!" I hear one of the baristas call out. I look up to see Daniel walking in the door, looking happy and relaxed. He smiles and gives a little wave to the girl behind the counter. I notice that he's moving a little slowly, but he seems in good spirits.

"Good morning," Daniel says. "I'd like the usual, please."

As the barista goes off to make Daniel's drink, I walk up behind him. "Mr. Jameson?" I say, tapping him lightly on the shoulder.

"Yes," he says, looking momentarily confused before breaking into a grin. "Would you be Charlotte?"

"I would," I say, extending my hand. "It's great to meet you."

"Likewise. And please call me Daniel," he says. His grip is surprisingly firm, and I'm hoping like hell he doesn't notice how much my hand is sweating.

"Will do," I say as the barista approaches and hands Daniel his drink. "What are you having?"

"Black coffee," Daniel says. "Ordering those fancy drinks takes longer than writing a novel."

"I'd like what he's having," I say to the barista, smiling. After I grab my coffee, Daniel and I settle into a table.

"Quinn tells me you want to introduce my work to a new generation," Daniel says. "That's quite a noble effort. But I can't imagine young people being interested in an old man and his books."

"Well, I can," I say, thinking of the students that showed up for his book signing. "And that's why I wanted to talk to you."

"All right," Daniel says, taking a sip of coffee. "Fire away."

"I understand that you studied journalism in college," I say. "So, you obviously knew you were going to be a writer."

"Hmm… not really," Daniel says. "I certainly *hoped* to be one. It was all I thought about. But I had serious doubts that I would ever be a real writer."

"That's unbelievable," I say. "With your talent, how could you envision yourself as anything other than that?"

"When you marry young, there are certain expectations," Daniel says. "One of which is a steady income to support your new bride."

"So, she wasn't working," I say.

"That was not an option," Daniel says. "Claire was quite focused on having children."

"And you had three sons," I say. Daniel nods, offering nothing more. Although I'm dying to probe further into his family dynamic, I can't have him shutting down on me this early in the game.

"So, what did you do to keep the lights on?"

"I went into field sales. Traveled quite a bit," Daniel says, starting to relax again. "Office supplies and equipment. Sold lots of typewriters, which should tell you how old I am." He smiles and gives me a little wink.

"I've had more than a few typewriters in my time, so let's not start talking about age," I say. "Did you like being out on the road?"

"You know, I actually did," Daniel says. "It could be lonely, but most of the time I enjoyed the solitude. Gave me time to think."

"And to write," I say.

Daniel nods. "I did some of my best work when I was camped out in a motel room," Daniel says. "I kept at that gig for about ten years. But even with commissions, it didn't pay enough. Certainly not as the boys got older."

"So, where did you land next?" I ask.

"Encanto & Associates," he says. "They hired me as an editor. I figured if I couldn't be one of the big shot authors, I could at least bask in their glow."

"You actually *worked* there?" I say. "I'll bet they freaked when they found out their next best-selling author was right under their nose."

Daniel winces almost imperceptibly. "It wasn't quite like that," he says. "The powers that be weren't terribly interested in helping my writing career. At least not without a significant amount of jumping through hoops on my part."

"But you kept on writing," I say.

"I couldn't stop. Though I tried at times," Daniel says. "But the muse will only let you ignore her for so long. Surrender is inevitable."

"I know," I say. "I mean… that makes sense for someone like you."

"Someone like *me*?" Daniel says. "You're a writer, too, you know."

"Well, yes," I say. "But most of the time I'm stuck at my day job. I just do these freelance pieces on the side."

"Doesn't matter," Daniel says, leaning forward. "Do words and ideas come to you uninvited? Do you feel like you have to write them down even if you don't know what good they'll ever do?"

"All the time," I say.

"Then you're no different than me," Daniel says.

"Except I haven't exactly written the great American novel."

"Do you want to?" Daniel asks.

"Well, I wanted a pony when I was six, but that didn't work out either," I say, wishing we could take the focus off my feeble attempts at a writing career.

"Answer the question."

"Wait a minute, who's interviewing who?" I say. Daniel just leans back with his arms crossed. "All right, yes. I would love to write a book. But—"

"Don't cancel a good intention with a lame excuse," Daniel says, cutting me off. "Now, when do you do most of your writing?"

"Nights and weekends," I say. "No, that's not really true. I sneak in most of my writing at work."

"I just told you I wrote my best stuff during work travel," Daniel laughs. "Great minds think alike."

"I know I shouldn't be doing my own work on the company dime. But sometimes I feel so swallowed up by the machine that I've got to stop and do something to remind myself that I'm not really a part of it," I say. "Or at least pretend that I'm not."

"You aren't, and you know it," Daniel says. "Which is why you need to be someplace where you actually *want* to belong."

"I don't think switching jobs is the answer," I say. "I'd feel like an alien at any company I worked for."

"I'm not talking about a new job," Daniel says. "I'm talking about a writers group. You need to join one."

"Actually, I found one," I say.

"And how is it?" Daniel asks.

"I haven't gone yet," I say. "I figure that I'm already great at criticizing the hell out of my own work, so do I really need a room full of people telling me that it sucks?"

"That's not what it's like," Daniel says. "Everyone is there to share their work and to support each other. And don't you think it'd be difficult to feel like an alien amongst your own kind?"

I shrug, knowing he's right. "Just *go*," Daniel continues. "Once. For me. Promise?"

"I'll go to the writers group if you let me get back on track with this interview," I say, smiling. "How's that?"

"Fair is fair," Daniel says. "I believe we left off somewhere between motels and the muse."

*

"I really wish you'd have been there," Rob says, practically bouncing around the kitchen while I'm making dinner. "I know you would've fallen in love with London within seconds, just like I did."

"*Seconds*?" I say. "That's a little over the top."

"No, it really isn't," Rob insists. "The city has over two thousand years of history behind it. Just incredible. There are buildings there that have existed longer than our country!"

"Since when are you an architecture nut?" I say.

"Since I found out my new office is in the second-tallest skyscraper in London," Rob says. "Fifty stories tall. The view is unbelievable!"

"Sounds awesome," I say. "Can you hand me the pepper grinder?"

Rob passes the pepper, not missing a beat in his hard sell. "You know, people always say English food is crap, but I had the most killer meals while I was there. Not a bad restaurant to be found."

"I'm pretty sure the unlimited expense account had something to do with that," I say. "No way Callerstrom was going to let his golden boy dine on pub grub."

"I looked at a few flats while I was there," Rob says, ignoring my snark. "I sent you the links, but you never responded. Did you get them?"

"I think I saw them in my inbox, but they must've gotten deleted before I had a chance to look at them," I say, focusing a little too intently on the pot of chili I'm cooking. The incessant talk of all things across the pond is making me lose my appetite.

"Well, let's pull them up now," Rob says. "Lemme go grab my laptop."

"I'm trying to finish making dinner," I say. "We can look later."

"It'll just take a second," Rob insists, dashing out of the kitchen and nearly stepping on Phoebe in the process.

"I know, girl. He's lost it," I say. "If he starts talking like Paul McCartney, you have my permission to bite him on the leg."

Rob returns with his laptop and plops it down on the counter. He taps a few keys then motions to the screen. "This is a really nice place in Notting Hill," he says.

"Like the Julia Roberts movie?"

"Yep!" Rob says. "And I think Hugh Grant actually lives there. We could be neighbors!"

"I'm sure he'll invite us over for tea and crumpets."

"Check out this one in Kensington," Rob says, clicking on another link.

"Who lives there? Sir Elton John?"

Rob snaps the laptop shut. "Why are you being so negative?" he says. I can tell he wants to use stronger words but is holding back to get me on board.

"I'm not being negative," I say. "I just asked if we could wait until after dinner for the real estate virtual tour and you completely ignored me."

"Well, maybe this is just a little more important than a bowl of chili," he says. "We can't keep avoiding this subject. Or more to the point, *you* can't."

I want to protest, but he's right. "Okay," I say. "I'm listening."

"Well, first off, I looked into Phoebe's issue," he says. "Turns out that dogs coming into London don't have to be quarantined as long as you follow certain protocol. Documentation, shots… stuff like that."

"Great," I say. But instead of relief, I feel a knot forming in my chest. I try to smile, but I'm pretty sure I just look constipated.

"I thought you'd be more excited about that," Rob says. "I mean, that was your main problem, right?"

"Yeah, it was a big one," I say, struggling to not add a "but" to the end of the sentence.

"Just think of it," Rob says. "You and Phoebe strolling through Hyde Park every day."

"Except when it's freezing cold and raining," I say before I can stop myself. "Which is most of the time."

"You can't be bothered to look at houses in London, but now you're their resident meteorologist?" Rob says.

I start to answer but realize that anything I say is going to ignite an argument. So, I turn my attention back to stirring the chili.

"I'm gonna go watch the game," Rob says, heading for the living room. I hear him mutter something sarcastic under his breath about me being so open-minded.

I look over at Phoebe, trying to imagine the idyllic scene that Rob painted. The two of us strolling through a world-famous park. Probably stopping for coffee at some cute cafe where I can people-watch and jot down story ideas. No office to rush back to. No cube farm politics to navigate.

I should be doing the Snoopy dance and packing like a mad woman. Buying new clothes and practicing being a glamorous expatriate. Instead, I'm fixated on a pot of beans and my latent anxiety. Something is definitely wrong. And I'm not sure I'm ready to face whatever it is.

Chapter Fifteen

When I walk into the kitchen, I see Rob rummaging through the fridge for something to make for breakfast. His laptop is perched on the counter and opened up to a document titled, "U.K. Expansion Plan." I look away, feeling a familiar lurch in my stomach. Rob emerges holding a carton of eggs and a bottle of orange juice.

"You look nice," he says, apparently in a forgiving mood after our standoff last night over British real estate. I have on a casual sundress instead of my usual jeans and t-shirt ensemble. "Have a hot date or something?"

"Sort of," I say. "I'm going to check out a writers group."

"What's that?" Rob asks, half-listening as he puts the eggs and juice on the countertop and meanders over to his laptop.

"It's where writers get together to support each other and talk about their craft," I say. "You can also have them critique your work."

"You want a bunch of strangers judging you?" Rob says.

"It's not *judging*. They're giving you constructive feedback," I say. "And hopefully they won't be strangers for long. I could use some new friends."

Rob starts to respond, but just nods and focuses his attention on his computer.

"What were you going to say?" I ask.

"That it's funny how new friends are great as long as they're in your own backyard," he says. "God forbid you should make some in another country."

"Do we really need to fight about this now?" I say.

"Who's fighting?" Rob says. "I'm just stating the obvious."

"What do you expect me to do?" I say. "Stop living my life until we're on a plane to England?"

"When it comes to anything remotely related to this job, I've learned to expect very little from you," Rob says, giving me a dismissive look before turning back to the expansion plan.

"I'm sorry," I say. "I didn't mean to snap at you."

"Just go have fun at your… whatever it is," Rob says, not looking up from his document.

I stand there for a moment, briefly considering staying home and trying to make amends with my husband. Asking him to tell me more about Callerstrom's plan for world domination and afternoons with Phoebe in Hyde Park.

But instead, I grab my purse and head out, knowing that he's not in the mood to talk and I've already kept my writing waiting long enough.

*

I haven't been in a library since college, and I've forgotten how peaceful it can be. Even though I'm nervous as hell to meet the people in the writers group, I feel a certain serenity when I walk through the doors that takes the edge off right away.

"Are you looking for the Scribe Tribe?"

I turn to see a woman in her late twenties with indigo-colored hair and a kind face decorated with several piercings and impossibly cool glasses. I suddenly feel very middle-aged.

"Yes," I say. "How did you know?"

"Because you have the same terrified-yet-excited look I had on my first day with the group," she says, smiling. "I'm Katya." She holds out her hand, and I shake it.

"Great to meet you, Katya," I say. "I'm Charlotte."

"Well, let's get in there," Katya says, motioning toward a door at the back of the library. "They'll be starting any minute. Did you bring your project?"

"All I've got at this point is notes," I say, following her. "Maybe I shouldn't have come until I had the first draft written."

"No, no!" Katya says. "I made that mistake. The earlier you get started with this bunch, the better. You can get a lot of awesome feedback and guidance before you even start drafting."

I nod, feeling grateful to her for taking me under her wing. As we enter the back room, I am relieved to see what I can only describe as a motley crew. There are people Katya's age and younger, as well as thirty- and forty-somethings on up to senior citizens. I feel my breathing begin to calm.

"Welcome, everybody! Take a seat!" bellows a large woman in a caftan with a head full of wild, flame-colored curls.

"Who's that?" I whisper to Katya.

"Our group leader, Roxanne," she says. "Actually, she's more like a moderator. Or a catalyst for insanity, depending on the day."

"Sort of marginally controlled creative bedlam," I say.

"Exactly!" Katya says. "Five minutes in and you've already got the lay of the land."

"Okay, let's get going!" Roxanne calls out. "But first I want to extend a warm welcome to those of you who are new to the Scribe Tribe."

Katya nudges me. "Stand up and introduce yourself!"

I shake my head, rooting myself further into my seat. My palms are sweating, and my heart is pounding, just like when I was a ten-year-old kid presenting a book report to my class. But this is fifty times worse because it's a book that *I'm* writing.

Katya stands up. "Roxanne, we have a new member," she says, motioning toward me. "Her name is Charlotte, and I just met her on the way into the library today."

Everyone turns in their seats to check out the cowering newbie. And for a moment, I am utterly mortified. But I start to relax when I see something in their eyes that isn't even close to the sneering judgment I was expecting: acceptance. I smile and rise to my feet.

"Hello, everyone," I say, my voice quavering slightly. "As you can tell, I'm a little—okay, a lot—nervous. But I'm very happy to be here. I have a lot to learn, so I'll be a good student."

"And a good teacher, as well," Roxanne says. "We all learn from each other. So glad you're here with us, Charlotte."

"Thank you so much," I say as I start to sink back into my chair.

"Now, don't you be sitting down just yet!" Roxanne says, eliciting a laugh from the crowd. "Tell us a little about yourself, and what you're working on."

"Well, I'm married with one four-legged child—my dog, Phoebe—and I work at a family law firm," I say. "I try to tell myself that I get a lot of great material from the place, with all the divorce drama going on. But honestly, it's just depressing." I have no idea why I'm turning a simple introduction into an episode of true confessions, but I can't seem to stop myself.

"Really? Do tell," Roxanne says.

"I don't belong there. I never have, and I don't ever want to," I say, my eyes starting to burn. "I want to write, but I'm afraid to let myself believe I can be the real deal."

"Why is that?" Roxanne asks.

"Because everything would change if I became who I'm supposed to be."

"And that scares you," Roxanne says.

"Yes," I say. "But not nearly as much as continuing to live the cube farm status quo."

"Then I'd say you're in the right place," Roxanne says. "So, tell us what you're writing these days."

"Well, I've had the good fortune to meet an amazingly talented author named Daniel Jameson," I say, noting that several of the heads in the room are nodding in recognition. "He's been out of the spotlight for a while now, but he has quite a life story. And I'm going to tell it."

Chapter Sixteen

"So, I finally went to the writers group," I tell Daniel as we sit down at our usual table at Cinnamon's. "I was freaked out at first, but I ended up loving it."

"Good for you, Charlotte," Daniel says. His words are enthusiastic, but his voice is flat. He seems exhausted.

"I'd like to have a project to be working on in the group," I say. "And I've been thinking that, instead of just writing an article about you, I would love to write your memoir."

"Well, then you'd better write fast," Daniel says, giving a little laugh that rapidly progresses to a raspy cough.

"What do you mean?" I say. It hasn't been that long since I saw him last, but his skin looks almost grayish now.

"These treatments they're giving me," he says. "They make me feel like hell."

"What treatments?" I say, steeling myself for confirmation of the diagnosis the reporter tried pulling out of Daniel during the interview.

"I thought maybe Quinn told you," he says. "I've got something going on in my bones."

"You mean, cancer?" I say, feeling my throat tightening the same way it did when Mom gave me her news.

Daniel nods. "Sarcoma something or other," he says. "I wish they'd just speak English."

"You're doing what the doctors are telling you to, right?" I say, panic tingeing my voice. Daniel picks up on it and smiles softly.

"Yes, I'm going along with the program," he says. "But I'm not sure how much good it'll do in the long run. Not that there is such a thing as a long run with something like this."

"Don't say that!" I snap, without meaning to. "I mean, there's a chance you can beat this, right?"

"There's always a chance of anything," Daniel says. "But right now, the white coats say that I'm not responding to therapy."

"Do they know why?" I ask.

Daniel shakes his head. "So, that means more tests and more drugs," he says. "Two of my least favorite things."

"You sound just like my mom did when she was sick," I say. "She hated feeling like a human guinea pig, with people hooking her up to machines and handing her a new pill every five minutes."

"They're just doing their jobs," Daniel says.

"I know. But it was tough to see her go through so much," I say. "How's your family handling all of this?"

"The boys are worried. All grown up and living out-of-state now, but they do check in on me," Daniel says. "They try to get me to do that Skype thing, but it's all I can do to figure out my damned cell phone." He gives a little chuckle.

"And what about your wife?" I ask.

Daniel stares down into his coffee cup, then looks away for a moment. "I'm fairly certain she thinks I deserve this."

"That's not funny," I say.

"No, it isn't," he says. "But it's true."

"How could she possibly feel that way?" I say. "You're her husband, for God's sake."

Daniel gives me a long look. "Claire is still punishing me for an affair I had over thirty years ago."

My heart almost stops. Even though I know all about the affair—or at least what Mom's mementos revealed—it's still a shock to hear him acknowledge it out loud.

"So, was it something casual?" I ask. "You know, just a fling." I feel my breath catch, anticipating an answer I might not want to hear.

"Not at all," Daniel says, his eyes softening. "She was an amazing lady. Very special to me."

I feel a wave of relief flooding my chest. "What made her so special?" I ask.

"So many things," he says. "Beautiful. Funny. But most of all, she made me feel like myself. I didn't have to perform, the way I did with Claire. Nothing I did was ever good enough for her…" he trails off, his face clouding.

"But you chose Claire over this woman," I say. "So, you must have loved her. Right?"

Daniel gives me a pained look. "Sometimes choices are based on love," he says. "Other times, fear and convenience take the lead."

"But you gave her what she wanted," I say. "You kept the family together. Maintained the status quo. So, why won't she forgive you after all this time?"

"How long have you been married, Charlotte?" he says.

"Almost eighteen years," I say.

"Then you've been married long enough to know that things aren't always so clear-cut. That forgiveness isn't always a given," he says. "And neither is the kind of love that would make you follow someone across the world."

"That's an interesting litmus test for devotion," I say.

"But it's a good one, don't you think?" Daniel says.

"Yeah, sure. I guess," I say.

"Would you follow your husband across the world?"

My throat suddenly feels dry. "Actually, I may have to," I say. "He's considering a position in London."

"*Have* to?" Daniel says, folding his arms across his chest.

"I didn't mean it that way," I say.

"But it's how you feel," he says. "Why don't you want to go? It's one of the most exciting cities in the world."

"You sound just like my husband," I say. "Rob is so geeked-out on the idea I can't get him to talk about anything else. He thinks he's going to have Prince William on speed dial."

"You still haven't answered my question," Daniel says. "Why don't you want to go?"

"I never said I didn't want to," I say, wondering how this conversation got completely turned around on me.

"Never mind. I'm sorry," Daniel says. "It's not my place to pry."

He's right. But I find myself answering anyway. "We haven't been getting along that well. It's not horrible all the time. Just not… great," I say. "I can handle it because I've got so many other distractions. But five thousand miles away…"

"You'd be forced to face your status quo," Daniel says.

I look down, but I feel Daniel's eyes on me. "I already have."

"No," he says. "I think you've given it a glance. Truly facing it requires making a decision one way or the other."

"Just like you did?" I say, meeting his gaze again.

"Yes. Exactly," he says. And for a moment, I can see the memories of my mother flickering behind his eyes.

*

I'm just back from lunch and preparing to kill off the rest of the day by updating files when I see Trina coming towards me with a grim look on her face.

"Can you come with me for a second?" she says. "Erica needs to speak with you."

"Sure," I say, trying to figure out what I could've done to incur Erica's wrath. Misfiled something? Offended a client? Made a pot of subpar coffee?

As we head down the hall, Trina makes an abrupt turn toward the employee lounge.

"I thought we were going to talk to—"

"SURPRISE!!!"

I nearly jump out of my skin when I see the entire firm standing there, surrounded by balloons and streamers, their heads adorned by ridiculous party hats. There is a huge cake from a very expensive local bakery and some equally pricey champagne. For a second, I think they've mistakenly thrown me a birthday party. That is, until I notice the giant banner hanging on the back wall: HAPPY 10th ANNIVERSARY CHARLOTTE!

"I, um… oh my God." Everyone is staring at me, their eyes lit up with anticipation of my joyous outburst. But I am completely mortified. Not just by the attention, but by the fact that I've been here for an entire decade.

"Okay, we need to make a toast!" Trina shrieks as she tries to wrestle the cork out of one of the bottles.

"You're gonna put someone's eye out with that," Will says, taking the bottle from her and releasing the cork with a festive pop. He grabs a glass, fills it and hands it to me.

"I'd wish you a happy anniversary, but I'm pretty sure you'd punch me in the face," Will says under his breath.

"Only if you promise to respond by knocking me over the head with one of those bottles," I say. "I'm pretty sure the paramedics could get me out of here in about ten minutes."

"Everybody listen!" Trina yells again, clinking a spoon against her glass. "Erica has a few words to say." All eyes turn toward our Versace-clad leader, and I try to mimic their anticipatory stares.

"When Charlotte first came to us, I thought she wouldn't last two months," Erica says. Everyone starts murmuring, unsure as to where this toast is going. "The front desk is an important job, but it can be thankless. Phones going crazy, and clients going even crazier." She's right on all counts. Two months would've been about the time that any sane person would've fled like her ass was on fire. So, I am officially more nuts than the phones and our clientele put together.

"But fortunately for us, Charlotte chose to stick it out and become a highly valued member of the Steiner Chase family," Erica continues. "And to show our appreciation, I have a little something for her." Trina hands Erica a small, beautifully wrapped box, which she then presents to me.

"Thank you," I say, carefully removing the ornate paper. When I lift the lid of the box, I see an engraved gold nameplate.

"It's beautiful," I say. "It'll look great on my desk."

"No, it won't," Erica says, grinning. "It's for your new office door."

"What?" I say as the minions start murmuring again, possibly as confused as I am.

"You've been on the front lines long enough," Erica says. "And Trina is absolutely swamped running this place. So, the partners have decided to promote you to assistant practice manager."

A cheer rises from the crowd, and everyone starts clapping. Trina bounds over and gives me a big hug, almost spilling both of our glasses. "I really didn't expect this," I say. "But… um… thank you very much."

"Well, you deserve it," Erica says, raising her glass. "Here's to Charlotte… and to another ten years!" Everyone clinks glasses and Trina starts cutting the cake. I look over at Will, and he shakes his head before downing his champagne like a shot.

"Kinda takes you by surprise, doesn't it?" Denise says, sidling up to me and touching her glass to mine.

"Well, yeah," I say. "I wasn't exactly expecting a promotion and a room full of screaming people wearing party hats when I got back from lunch."

"Actually, I meant the years," Denise says. "You start here, and the next thing you know, ten or twenty of them have flown by. My twenty-fifth anniversary will be coming up pretty soon."

"Wow," I say, not entirely sure if she's proud or simply resigned. "Congratulations."

"It is what it is," she says, shrugging. "Beats unemployment."

I nod, feeling like a complete fake. I should be happy about the new role and the new office. More money, more privacy… what's not to like? But as I look around the room at everyone smiling and chatting, it's obvious that they have a sense of contentment that I don't. Even with her constant bitching and flinty demeanor, Denise exudes a feeling of comfort with her station at the firm. And even though Erica pronounced me part of the family, it's clear to me that I'm the red-headed stepchild.

*

"So, what do you think?" Abby says as she shows me and Rob around her new condo, weaving her way through the throng of people here to celebrate her housewarming.

"It's gorgeous," I say. The décor is as beautifully eclectic as she is. "I'd give anything for your sense of style."

"It's sort of Restoration Hardware bastardized by Ikea, but it works for me," Abby says. "All right, time to get you two some adult beverages."

"No argument here," Rob says as Abby leads us toward a makeshift bar where several people are mixing their own concoctions. I see Abby's face light up, and she makes a beeline for a ridiculously hip-looking couple. They're at least a decade younger than Rob and I, and the woman reminds me a little of Katya.

"Gina and Joe, meet Rob and Charlotte," Abby says. After we all shake hands and exchange pleasantries, Gina turns her attention to me. "Abby has told me so much about you. She says that you're a writer. Me, too!"

"Well, yeah. I mean, not full-time," I say, giving Abby the stink eye as she pretends not to see me. "I work at a law firm."

"What kinds of things do you write?" Gina asks, blowing right past my day job. She seems genuinely interested, which makes me even more self-conscious.

"Mostly short stories and essays," I say. "But I never really got anywhere with them. So, I just joined a writers group, and I'm working on my first book."

"That's awesome!" Gina says. "What's it about?"

"Actually, it's the memoir of an author friend of mine," I say. "What sort of writing do you do?"

"Mostly novels," she says. "Joe goofs on them for being *chick lit.*"

"Hey, I stopped goofing after you blew up on Amazon. Two-time bestseller and counting," he says, smiling. "And tell them about the movie deal."

"A *movie*? How could I not know about this?" Abby says.

"Nothing is set in stone," Gina says. "An indie producer read one of my books and really liked it. He wants me to write the screenplay adaptation, and we'll see where it goes from there."

"That's incredible," I say, wanting to sink through the floor. "Congratulations."

"Aw… thanks so much," she says. "When will your book be done? I love a good memoir."

"I'm not sure," I say. "I just got a promotion to assistant practice manager at the firm, so I don't have time to write as much as I'd like to."

"Well, that's likely to change," Rob says. "I've been offered a position at my company that would take us to the U.K. I'll be running their new office in London. Huge enough step up that Char won't have to work."

"I love England!" Gina says. "We honeymooned in London."

Rob puts his arm around me. "So, you can play around with your writing all you want to," he says. "No need for two starving artists in the same house, right?"

Joe, Gina and my globetrotting husband immediately launch into a discussion about all things British, as Abby's jaw drops. I stare down into my drink, avoiding her eyes. I know I should've told her this was on the table, but I still can't face it myself. And I'm starting to wonder if I'll ever be able to.

Chapter Seventeen

I'm at our usual table at Cinnamon's, waiting for Daniel and organizing my notes for today's interview session when I see him shamble in. He gives the barista a little smile as he collects his cup of coffee, but I can tell he's in pain. I feel more than a little guilty that he's dragged himself here when he feels so awful.

"How are you holding up?" I ask as he sits down across from me.

"I'm all right," he says, wincing slightly as he adjusts himself in his chair.

"Listen, we can do this another time," I say. "I'm sure you'd rather be home relaxing."

Daniel shakes his head. "Actually, I'm glad to get the hell out of the house," he says. "I don't find it to be much of a sanctuary these days." I wait for him to elaborate further, but he doesn't.

"I'm sorry to hear that," I say. "Still, we can put this off if you aren't up to it."

"To be honest, I'm in more of a listening mood today," Daniel says. "Tell me about what you've been up to."

"Well, I had quite the week at the day job," I say.

"Let's hear it," Daniel says.

"It was my ten-year anniversary at the firm," I say. "They gave me this huge surprise party and a promotion. But I just felt like I wanted to run for the hills."

"And why is that?" Daniel asks, though I'm sure he already knows.

"Because I want to be as happy as everyone else is to be there," I say. "But I'm not."

"How do you know they're happy?" Daniel says. "They obviously think you are, and look how off the mark they were."

"Good point," I say.

"And let me guess… you feel guilty because you weren't grateful enough for the gift that was bestowed upon you," he says.

"Exactly."

"You don't have to want something just because it's given to you," Daniel says. "Or compromise your dreams to settle for what seems practical."

"I just feel like I've wasted so much time," I say. "And that I'm delusional to think I could become a real writer at this stage of the game."

"I hit my biggest literary stride in my forties. As my biographer, you should know this," Daniel says, giving me a wink. "So, what's stopping you from just leaving behind what no longer serves you?"

"You mean quit the firm?" I ask. "And do what? Follow Rob to England and learn to make bangers and mash, or whatever the hell they eat over there?"

"I wasn't aware that was the only option besides corporate servitude," Daniel says.

"Look, there's a lot to consider before I jump ship," I say. "I can't pay my bills with artistic angst."

Daniel gives me a long look, then breaks into a grin. "You're facing your status quo," he says. "And it appears to be scaring the hell out of you."

"I really want to tell you that you're full of shit," I say. "But you're right."

"At the risk of sounding arrogant, I think I am," he says.

"But there's nothing really wrong with my life," I say. "So, maybe it's *me* that's the problem. I don't want to be that person who's always thinking there's something better around the corner," I say.

"But what if there is?" Daniel says. "Don't you owe it to yourself to find out?"

"How can I do that without blowing up everything I have?" I say.

Daniel shrugs. "I can't help you with that, my dear," he says. "But let me tell you, I have missed out on more 'something betters' than I care to recall."

He reaches for his coffee and takes a sip, his voice breaking slightly as he continues.

"And I don't want that for you," he says. "Not in any way whatsoever."

*

"Thanks for being okay with doing lunch here again," Will says, handing me an iced tea from his tiny studio refrigerator. "Not exactly Trask's, but at least the walls don't have ears."

"You didn't seem concerned about that before," I say, my eyes scanning the walls filled with his newest batch of photos. I can't help but notice how much he's improving, and I feel a sense of admiration for both him and his work. It makes me ache to get back to Scribe Tribe.

"Yeah, well, I can't have office Blab Squad hearing what I have to tell you," he says. "At least not yet."

"Okay, you're freaking me out a little," I say. "What's wrong?"

"Nothing. Actually, it's something that feels very right," he says. "I'm leaving Shelly. And I'm going to have Erica represent me."

"*What*?" I say. "Aren't you at least going to try to work it out? I mean, for the kids."

Will shakes his head. "I've tried enough. Jumped through every fucking hoop, until I practically forgot who I was," he says. "And I have you to thank for reminding me."

"I didn't do anything," I say.

"Yes, you did," Will says. "You didn't laugh at me when I showed you my photos, for starters."

"Why would I?" I say. "They're amazing."

"So was that night at Trask's," he says. "Or am I the only one who thought so?"

"It was nice," I said. "But it shouldn't have happened."

"But it did," he says. "And I'm glad. Because the feelings I let myself have for you were a wake-up call."

"Whoa, wait a second," I say. "Please don't tell me I had anything to do with the decision to blow up your marriage."

"I was miserable with Shelly for a long time before we had our *moment*, or whatever you want to call it," Will says. "But it reminded me of what I've been missing."

"I'm not sure what to say to that."

"How about that you'll still be my friend?" Will says. I can tell he wants to reach for my hand, but he instead folds his in his lap.

"Of course," I say. "How would I survive at the firm without you?"

"I wasn't talking about us being office buddies," Will says. "I thought maybe we connected over more than just spreadsheets and shitty coffee."

"We did. I mean, we *do*," I say. "We both have dreams that have gotten buried under the behemoth known as 'responsible adulthood.'"

"And we both have spouses that don't seem to give a damn about that," he says.

"Well, apparently you won't have one for long," I say.

"And you?"

"I never said I was leaving Rob," I say, instantly regretting my wine-fueled over-sharing at the bar. "Just because he's not—"

Will holds up his hand. "I'm sorry. That was totally out of line," he says. "I just want you to be happy."

"But you're not properly convinced that I am," I say. "Don't worry about me."

"Can't help it," he says. "But the fact is, I want you in my life. On whatever terms you'll give me."

I nod, knowing that I have no idea what the blueprint of our so-called friendship looks like going forward. But I do know that tumbling into an affair with a fellow thwarted artist is no panacea for the fear and self-doubt I've harbored for much too long.

"We've got to get back to the office," I say. "There's something I need to take care of."

*

"Are you busy?" Trina asks, popping her head into my office. She never bothers to ask if I'm busy before barreling in with her arms loaded with work or some crazy client anecdote that can't wait. So, I'm instantly wary.

"I'm working on the Delano case, but I'm not swamped." Actually, I've been staring at a blank screen since I got back from lunch two hours ago. "Come on in."

"So, how *are* you?" Trina asks, a weird hesitancy tingeing her voice as she sits down across from my desk.

"Fine. Same as always," I say. "Why are you looking at me like that?"

"Like what?"

"Like I'm on the verge of a psychotic break," I say.

"Sorry, I just… well, I know this new position comes with a lot of pressure," she says. "I just want to make sure it's not too much for you."

"Have you forgotten where we work?" I say. "Pressure is as prevalent as black coffee and Xanax. Why the sudden concern?"

Trina goes silent for a long moment, clearly laboring to script something in her head before she spits it out. As I sit there watching her struggle, I hear Will laughing in the hallway with one of his buddies.

"He told you, didn't he?"

"Huh? I mean, who told me what?" Trina stammers.

"Will told you that he's leaving his wife, and he wants the firm to represent him in the divorce," I say. "And let me guess, he just happened to mention that he wasn't the only one fresh out of marital bliss."

"Please don't be mad at him," Trina pleads. "He just wants to make sure you're taken care of."

"What the hell does that mean?" I say. "Taken care of *how*?"

"Well, if you were to need… you know…"

"No, actually I *don't* know," I say. "What exactly did he say to you?"

Trina looks like she wants to sink through the floor. "He said that he thinks you're unhappy at home, but you're too afraid to… um… explore your options."

"Are you kidding me?" I say. "He has no right to speculate on my marriage, let alone talk to you about it!"

"I'm so sorry," Trina says. "I shouldn't have said anything."

"It's not your fault," I say. "But Will should've kept his opinions to himself."

"His intentions were good," she says. "He really cares about you."

"That's no excuse."

"Maybe so," Trina says. "But now that the proverbial cat is out of the bag, is there anything I can help you with? If you don't want to talk to anyone at the firm, there are other resources I can connect you with."

"There is no cat, and there is no bag," I say. "I appreciate your concern, but it's completely unfounded."

"Understood," Trina says, getting up and turning toward the door. "But if you change your mind, just let me know."

"Will do."

As Trina leaves, I turn back toward my blank screen. My gut is churning, but I am finally ready to write what I know that I need to:

Dear Erica,

It is with much regret that after ten years of service, I will be leaving Steiner Chase & Associates…

Chapter Eighteen

"So, when were you going to fill me in on your impending exodus to Britain?" Abby says as we sit down at our table at Cinnamon's.

"I'm sorry. And I know I have no excuse," I say. "But I guess I haven't really been able to face it myself. And telling you about it would've meant it was real."

"Well, it's not like I'm excited about my best friend fleeing the country," Abby says. "But I understand. It's a huge career leap for Rob, and London is an amazing city."

"If one more person tries to school me on how fabulous London is, I'm going to move there just so I can dive headfirst off of Big Ben."

"Oh, come on!" Abby says. "You can quit your shitty day job and live life as an author overseas. That's every writer's dream!"

"Well, maybe it isn't mine," I say, taking a sip of my coffee. "Ugh. This is ice cold. I need a warm up. Be right back."

"Nice try," Abby says, putting her hand on my arm as I start to get up. "Sit your nitpicky ass down and talk to me."

I flop back into my chair. "I don't know what's wrong with me," I say. "I'm a total idiot. I should be ecstatic."

"Yes, you should," Abby says. "But you're not. So, what gives?"

"Well, first off, there's Phoebe," I say. "I can't see putting her through a move like that. And don't tell me she's 'just a dog' and she'll be fine."

"I value my life too much to utter those words," Abby says. "But you and I both know, you'd charter a damn private jet to get her there safely if you had to. So, moving on to the next excuse. And if it involves any kind of loyalty to that legal dungeon you work in, I will not be responsible for my actions."

"Actually, I wrote my resignation letter the other day," I say. "I haven't turned it in yet. And maybe I shouldn't."

"Are you kidding me? Of course you should!" Abby says. "Talk about divine timing. You finally get fed up with that place, and boom! Rob rolls out the financial red carpet. Perfect!"

"Yeah," I say. "But the carpet is in England."

"So is your husband," Abby says.

"And no one else."

"Not for long. You'll meet new friends," Abby says. "Though none as amazing as me, of course."

I nod, trying to smile. "But I just started with my writing group here."

"You'll find another one."

"And they drive on the wrong side of the road over there," I say. "I'll probably end up causing a three-car pileup my first day in town."

Abby stares at me. "Any other dire prognostications, Susie Sunshine?"

"Excuse me for not being thrilled about uprooting my entire life," I say.

"I get it," Abby says. "But as much as Rob is in love with the idea of being Mr. International Businessman, I guarantee you he's nervous, too."

I shake my head. "If teleporting was an option, he'd be there yesterday."

"And maybe that's a good thing," Abby says. "Since he's not the one that's freaked out, he'll be able to help you settle in. Nice and smooth."

"I'm not so sure about that."

Abby slaps her forehead with her palm. "You're talking in circles," she says. "Please either tell me what's really going on, or that it's none of my business."

"All right. It's not just the move I'm worried about," I say. "Rob and I haven't been getting along all that great for a while now."

"Shit," Abby says. "I had no idea."

"I think I started feeling the distance around the time Mom passed," I say. "The day that he didn't want to go into her room at the hospice with me, I remember there was this... I don't know, numbness in my heart. Like, this isn't the guy I married."

"Everyone handles that stuff differently," Abby says. "I'd like to think I'd have been there for you, but I've been known to flee a hospital or six in my time."

"I know. And I tried to turn it back on myself," I say. "Like I was just upset because Mom was so sick. But there was more to it. We weren't 'us' anymore."

"Does Rob have any idea you feel this way?" Abby says.

I shrug. "If he does, he never says anything," I say. "Then again, neither do I."

"Well, that's wildly productive," Abby says. "If he has no clue that anything is wrong, how do you expect him to change?"

"Maybe I don't," I say.

"What do you mean?"

"Rob's career has always taken center stage," I say. "And I was fine with that because I told myself that he was the genius. The businessman. The one whose talent was the kind that made money in the world."

"And yours isn't?" Abby says.

"I never believed it was," I say. "So, I thought it would be enough to just be his wife and just tinker with writing on the side. If I made something of it, great. If not, I'd still have a good life."

"But not one that was really your own," Abby says.

I nod. "But I've realized that I don't want to just write," I say. "I want to live the whole life that goes with putting words into the world. The freedom. The community with other writers. Doing the work until the day comes where I can say *I'm an author* and not want to crawl into a hole."

"Or a cubicle," Abby says.

"Amen to that," I say. "But I don't think Rob understands. And it's not his fault because I let him think that our status quo was just fine. Because I really wanted it to be."

"Well, what do you want now?" Abby says.

"To be as excited about my life as Rob seems to be about his."

"Well, then maybe this move will be just what you need," Abby says. "It'll be a new start for both of you. And for your marriage."

"But what if it's not?" I say. "I'll be halfway across the world. It's not like I can just pack up and wing it back here."

"You haven't even pulled out a suitcase, and you're already talking about coming back," Abby says.

"Because I'm scared, all right?" I say. "This move has made me question why Rob and I have made it this far. And sometimes I think it's simply because we've got all of our comfy little buffers in place: jobs, friends, routines. But it's pretty difficult to ignore the charade when you're in a place where nothing and no one is familiar."

"Pretty high stakes," Abby says.

"I could lose everything," I say. "And the weird thing is, a part of me wonders if that wouldn't be the worst thing in the world."

*

I've got another meeting with Scribe Tribe in a few days, so I'm really feeling the pressure to make some decent progress on my project. But today, the words just aren't coming, and I find myself looking for any kind of distraction to avoid the continual dance with the blank page. Out of the corner of my eye, I see Phoebe nosing around the box of Mom's stuff, and I take that as a divine sign that I'm due for a break.

"How about I just chalk this up to research instead of slacking?" I ask Phoebe, who flops down on the floor in response. As I dig through the contents, I realize that there are actually a few books in the box that I'd meant to take a look at. But I've been so preoccupied with what I could uncover in her journals that I haven't really given them any attention. I scoop a few of them up and sit down next to Phoebe.

Not surprisingly, there are a couple books of poetry and a short story anthology. But there is one with a plain beige cover toward the bottom of the stack that almost escapes my attention. But as soon as I see the title, the rest of the volumes in my lap are quickly forgotten.

Breaking the Wheelhouse—First Draft

As I open it up, I see that it isn't just any copy of the initial version of Daniel's bestseller. It's literally the very first draft he wrote, complete with notes in the margins and red pen markings all over the place. And he had it bound just for my mother.

I look at the inside cover, and there is a short inscription from Daniel:

Here's hoping this is worth something one day. But even if it's not, I hope you know that you're the reason it exists. You're my heart and everything in it.

Always,

Daniel

I begin turning the pages, looking for other notes from Daniel. I'm curious to see not only if he wrote anything else to Mom, but what his notes to himself were about the book that would eventually make him famous.

But Daniel's words to my mother are quickly forgotten as I turn each page, uncovering something that brings fresh tears to my eyes.

My mother had filled this book with notes of her own. Jotted on scraps of paper and tucked neatly between almost every page are dozens of ideas for stories she wanted to write. Wisdom she ached to share. Characters she longed to bring to life.

Her visions and dreams were everywhere except where they needed to be most of all. In books with her name on them, to be shared with the world.

*

"Sorry I had you drive all the way over here," Daniel says as I follow him from the entryway to his kitchen. "I'm just not up to being out and about today." He looks even worse than the last time I saw him. His weight is down, and his eyes and cheeks are sunken.

"I'd have totally understood if you canceled," I say. "But I'm glad I'm here. How are you feeling?"

Daniel doesn't answer. Instead, he grabs two mugs and starts to pour the coffee. His hands are shaking so badly that he almost drops the pot on the countertop.

"Here, let me get it," I say, taking the pot from him as he grimaces in frustration. I pour the coffee, and we head out to the patio.

"So, what are the doctors saying about your progress?" I ask.

"I wouldn't know," Daniel says. "We're not on speaking terms these days."

"What do you mean?"

"That I'm done being their lab rat," he says. "I've stopped all treatments."

"You can't do that!" I say. "I mean… why?"

"Nothing was working anyway," Daniel says. "But God forbid the white coats would ever admit it. There was always one more pill, one more scan. One more test they wanted to try."

"But enough is enough," I say.

Daniel nods. "I was going to let you know," he says. "But I didn't want to upset you."

"It's okay," I say. "I understand."

"I'm perfectly fine with ditching this earth suit when it's time," Daniel says. But the hardest thing is knowing how much the ones that love you will be hurting when you're gone."

"I think that's why my mom hung on so long," I say. "For me."

"She sounds like a wonderful woman," Daniel says.

"The best," I say. "If she loved you, it was with every bit of her heart. No matter the cost."

"Is there any other way to do it?" Daniel says. "Anything less is a waste."

"That's what I always thought," I say. "But the person she loved the most—that she wanted to spend her life with—didn't return the favor."

"Your father?" Daniel says. "I take it they were divorced."

"I wasn't talking about my dad," I say. "And yes, they did divorce, but it wasn't his idea. It was Mom's. She was madly in love with someone else."

"I see," Daniel says. "And did she end up with this someone?"

"Not in the way she would've preferred," I say. "He had a wife and young children."

I think I see a bit of recollection flickering in Daniel's eyes. "So, they had…"

"An affair," I finish for him. "A big, crazy, passionate one that went on for several years. She really thought he'd leave his wife."

"And she just waited for him all that time," Daniel says.

I nod. "I don't know if he ever made any promises," I say. "All I have to go on is what I could piece together from her journals. But whatever they shared was enough to fuel her hope that they'd be together one day. And to crush her when that didn't happen."

"Well, it sounds like her gentleman friend wasn't remotely worthy of her," Daniel says. "Did you ever meet him?"

I feel my chest constricting, but I continue. "Yes, I did," I say. "Not long ago, actually."

"And what did you think of him?" Daniel asks. "Can't imagine it was much of anything positive."

"I didn't think it would be," I say. "But after spending some time with him, I started to see why she fell for him."

"Let me guess," Daniel says. "Handsome, witty, successful?"

"More than that," I say. "He sees the potential in everyone. Cuts right through your bullshit excuses as to why you can't be who you really are, or who you want to become. Mom needed that. I think when she was with him, she was truly herself. Maybe for the first time in her life."

Daniel leans forward, motioning for me to go on. "My father never wanted her to be anything more than a wife and mother," I say. "And while she was happy to be those things, that's not all she was. This man made her see that, and she loved him for it."

"But you don't think he loved her in return," Daniel says.

"I don't know," I say. "I need to ask him."

I reach into my purse and pull out the picture of Mom and Daniel kissing. I slide it gently across the table toward him.

"So, did you?"

Daniel's eyes widen, then fill with tears. "My God…"

"I wanted to tell you," I say, my own eyes welling up. "But I didn't know how or when to do it."

"So, you saying that you wanted to write about me was just a ploy to face off with the jerk that broke your mother's heart?" Daniel asks.

"It started out that way," I say. "After she died, her friend gave me a box of things Mom had left at her place. Almost every one of them had something to do with you. Pictures, notes… journals filled with poems and thoughts about your time together."

Daniel turns the photo over in his hands, reading the inscription on the back. "The Dolphin," he whispers. "She was right. It was definitely 'our place.' I loved coming up there to write with her by my side."

"Did Claire know about the Dolphin?" I ask.

Daniel shrugs. "Probably. But I didn't know or care. Whenever we were there, it was like I'd left the world and all its nonsense behind," he says. "I had my book and my Beth. That was all I needed."

"I think that's how Mom felt, too," I say.

Daniel stares down into his coffee cup. "I told Beth I wanted to marry her someday," he says. "I meant it."

"And she believed you," I say.

"Not at first, she didn't," Daniel says. "So, one day we went into town for an arts fair that was going on. There was this woman with a tiny table set up, dwarfed by the bigger tents and displays around her. Beth wandered over to look at what she had, and it was just one small tray of rings. Nothing very ornate, just some little diamond bands. I wasn't even sure the stones were real. But Beth seemed drawn to them."

"So, you bought her one," I whisper.

"Got down on one knee right there on the spot," Daniel says. "I was a fool in love. Had no business making a promise like that. But I told myself that someday I'd make good on it."

I look down at my right hand and start to feel dizzy. I pull the delicate sparkling band from my finger and hold it out to Daniel.

"And this was supposed to remind her of that promise?" I say.

Daniel takes the ring from me, holding it in his palm like a fragile bird. "I'd noticed your ring before, but there are a million ones just like it in the world," he says. "Who'd have ever guessed it was the one I gave my sweet Beth."

"She wore it all the time," I say. "And she put it on my finger right before she passed."

Daniel shakes his head slowly, handing the ring back to me. "I can't believe she kept it," he says. "Any other woman would've thrown it in the trash. God knows Claire would have."

"I still don't know why Claire didn't kick you out," I say. "She knew what was going on, and maybe even *where* it was going on. So, why didn't she just divorce you and take half of everything?"

"That's a logical question," Daniel says. "But we're talking about an illogical woman." His face darkens, and I can see his breathing becoming more rapid and shallow.

"Are you alright?" I say.

Daniel waves me off. "It was all about control with Claire," he says. "Watching me squirm was infinitely more rewarding than playing the martyred, cheated-upon wife in divorce court."

"You don't strike me as someone who's easily oppressed," I say.

"And you'd be correct," Daniel says. "But it was a different time. I was… not the same man." His knuckles are turning white as he grips his mug.

"It's okay," I say. "We don't have to talk about this right now."

"Yes, we do, goddammit," he says, as he begins coughing. I grab a glass of water, knowing it probably isn't going to help.

"Here, just take a drink," I say, wondering if I should call 911.

He swats the glass away and gets up, staggering toward the bathroom. I start to go after him, but sit back down instead, listening as he dry-heaves behind the closed door.

There's so much more we need to talk about. So much I want to tell him. My visit with Marnie. The baby. But right now, he's overwhelmed by having rediscovered my mother only to lose her all over again.

Today clearly isn't the day to push for answers, but I don't know how many more tomorrows Daniel has left. I still have so many questions. Please, God, let there be time for me to ask them.

Chapter Nineteen

"All right, Charlotte," Roxanne calls out from the front of the room. "Your turn!"

It's just a regular Scribe Tribe meeting, with all of us giving updates on our projects and sharing bits of them for critique. We've all become friends, so I've gotten over my initial fear of speaking in front of the group. But today, as I prepare to address everyone, I feel my knees shaking and my stomach doing flips.

"Are you okay?" Katya whispers as I start to stand up. "You look like you're going to pass out."

"I'm fine," I say. "Just a little off today, I guess."

"So, bring us up to speed on your book," Roxanne says. "Making good progress?"

"Fairly decent," I say. "But Daniel hasn't been feeling well lately, so it's made meeting with him more difficult."

"Ah, I'm sorry to hear that," Roxanne says. "Is he going to be all right?"

I start to offer assurances that he's going to be fine, but the words stick in my throat.

"I don't think so," I say. "He's very sick. Cancer."

The group begins murmuring, and Roxanne holds up her hand as a signal for them to quiet down and me to continue.

"The truth is, I've thought more than once about giving up on this book," I say. "A part of me wants to tell his story. But another part says that it's too hard on him to talk about his past. That I'm selfishly pushing this forward for my own gain."

"Do you really think that giving up is going to help him?" Roxanne asks. "Your interest in his life may be what's keeping him going."

"I'd like to believe that," I say. "Because I know I can't quit, even if I want to. And here's why."

I reach down into my tote bag and pull out Mom's copy of *Wheelhouse*. "This was one of my mother's very favorite books. She passed away not long before I joined the Tribe."

"I'm so sorry," Roxanne says. I feel Katya's eyes on me as she lets out a little gasp.

"As some of you may know, *Breaking the Wheelhouse* was Daniel's debut novel, and his most successful one," I say. "When I started this project, I thought that would be the focus. A pretty straightforward chronicle of his rise to fame as an author. But in our short time together, I've come to know that there was so much more to him than just his work."

"Sounds like he's become a friend as well as a subject," Roxanne says.

I nod. "Daniel is a wonderful man, but he never felt loved for anything other than what he could give. His readers loved him for his words, his publisher for his profitability, and his wife for the lifestyle he provided their family," I say. "But there was one woman who accepted and adored him for all that he was, and they shared several beautiful years together. But he kept their love to himself, and out of the public eye."

"Ah… a secret affair," Roxanne says, savoring the gossipy tidbit. "Is it someone we would know?"

"No. But I would," I say. "She was my mother."

The Tribe erupts, chattering loudly amongst themselves while Roxanne tries to regain control of the group. Finally, they settle down, and everyone sits silently, staring at me.

"Wow, you are certainly full of surprises today," Roxanne says.

"So was Mom," I say. "When she died, she left behind a box of mementos that documented her relationship with Daniel. Photos of the two of them, her journals… and this book."

I open up the novel and flip through the pages, showing them to the group. "This is the first draft of *Wheelhouse*, and Daniel had it bound for my mother," I say. "Which was appropriate, because he wrote it during their time together. It was for her. It was *about* her."

"She was his muse," Roxanne says quietly, shaking her head.

"I wasn't going to include their affair in my book, but Daniel insisted," I say. "He felt that he'd been living a lie until he met my mother. And he wants his memoir to be as real as the love they shared."

Roxanne nods her head as the group begins buzzing again. "Well, this is a story we all want to hear," she says. "And something tells me others will, too."

"I hope so," I say. "Because it's the story I was born to write."

*

When I walk in the door, I know immediately that something is off. Rob's car is in the garage, but I don't hear Phoebe's familiar welcome home yapping or her nails skittering on the tile as she races to meet me.

"Rob?"

As I begin heading towards our bedroom, I notice a pile of luggage in the middle of the living room. I walk closer to it, and I can see that each of the bags is covered in the familiar LV logo.

"So, what do you think? Nice, right?"

I turn around and see Rob standing there with a huge grin on his face. "Where's Phoebe?" I ask.

"In the backyard," he says. "She kept trying to eat the new luggage that you don't seem to give a damn about."

"Excuse me for being more than a little surprised to find six hundred pounds of Louis Vuitton in the middle of the living room," I say. "What's going on?"

"It's time for an upgrade," Rob says. "I'm not flying into London with beat up, crappy old bags."

"Fine," I say. "But this stuff is insanely expensive."

"Hold on a second," he says, turning to grab a small pile of papers off of the coffee table. "I think this will explain why money is no object."

I take the papers from him and begin to leaf through them. It's an employment contract, complete with a salary at the upper end of six-figures, a commission structure and a huge signing bonus. And it has Rob's signature on it.

"So, it's a done deal," I say.

"Look, you never said yes," Rob says. "But you also didn't say no. And Callerstrom finally told me that he'd have to move on to another candidate if I wouldn't commit."

"I understand," I say.

"Good," Rob says. "Glad you're finally on board."

"I said that I understand. And I do," I say, feeling my throat closing around the words I know I have to speak. "But I'm not on board. I can't go with you, Rob."

"What the hell are you talking about?" he says.

"Callerstrom's right," I say. "If someone can't commit, you have to move on. And I've got no right to keep you from something that you want so much."

"What, are you a pod person?" he says. "Where's all this 'I can't hold you back' bullshit coming from?"

"It's coming from me," I say. "And I've been feeling it for a while now. If I go, it won't be for the right reasons, and you'll resent me for it in the long run."

"Well, your timing is fantastic," Rob says, motioning to the pile of luggage. "How selfless of you to not stand in the way of me making us millionaires."

"It's not about the money," I say. "It's about you and me."

"No. It's about *you* being scared to get out of your goddamned comfort zone," Rob says.

"You're right, to some extent," I say. "But—"

"But, nothing. The only way out is through," he says. "You're afraid to make a move, but you've got to do it anyway." He grabs one of the smaller suitcases and heads down the hallway.

As I follow him into our bedroom, he throws the luggage on the bed, opens it up and starts grabbing my clothes from the closet. "I know what you're doing," I say. "But please stop it. I'm not one of your corporate minions who just needs a pep talk."

"At least they listen to reason," Rob says, throwing a few of my blouses into the suitcase.

"And just exactly how does you ransacking my closet constitute *reason*?" I say.

"Maybe it doesn't," Rob says. "But I finally got your attention. Which has been in pretty fucking short supply when it comes to discussing the move."

"I know. And I'm sorry," I say, sitting down on the bed.

"What exactly are you so terrified to leave behind?" Rob says. "Your job sucks, and it's not like you and Abby see each other every day. And you can find another writing club, or whatever it is. This is a chance to start over, Char."

I nod, feeling my pulse throb in my temples. "It is a chance to start over. For you, and for me," I say. "But not for us together."

"So, it's gonna be me in London and you here with Phoebe?" Rob says. "And, what, we see each other for birthdays and Christmas?"

"No," I say. "I want a divorce."

Rob shakes his head and lets out a derisive chuckle. "You want to end our marriage because the *dog* might rack up some flyer miles?" he says.

"It's more than that, and you know it."

"I don't know *anything* anymore when it comes to you," Rob says.

"And that's exactly my point," I say. "We stopped knowing each other a long time ago."

"Bullshit. We've been fine up until this whole moving thing," Rob says.

"Have we really?" I say. "When was the last time we laughed? Or went away for the weekend? Or even sat on the same end of the couch?"

"You sound like a character from one of those god-awful chick flicks," he says. "I thought that hanging out in that stupid coffee klatch would help you write better dialogue than that."

"It's called the Scribe Tribe," I say. "And it's not stupid. In fact, it's the one thing that made me realize what I really want. And to face the fact that I haven't had the guts to admit it to anyone, not even you."

Rob just stares at me, so I continue. "I want to be a writer," I say. "And I want it to be my whole life. Just like your work is to you."

"So, it's *my* fault that I'm doing what I want to, and you're not?"

"No, it's mine," I say. "I thought I could just make your dream my own. And I really wanted to. But I can't."

"Great," Rob says, crossing his arms in front of his chest. "So, now you've decided that your entire life is passing you by, and you need to go find your inner child in an ashram or have a midlife crisis or… fuck, I don't know."

"Don't make a joke out of this."

"Why not? That's exactly what this conversation is," Rob says. "You need to think about this long and hard."

"I've done nothing but that," I say. "For years now."

"Well, then one more night of consideration won't kill you," Rob says, turning and stomping out of the room. I follow him down the hall.

"Where are you going?"

"I don't know," he says, grabbing his car keys off the entryway table. "But I'm not staying here tonight."

As the door slams behind him, hot tears stream down my cheeks. I hear a scratching sound, and turn to see Phoebe pawing at the patio door. I run over and let her in, burying my face in her fur.

"Why can't I just want a nice normal life, with a nice normal husband?" I whisper.

I look across the room to a framed photo of Mom. She is dressed in her work suit, beaming with joy. It was her first day at Encanto. The day she began creating her own new normal. I wipe my eyes and reach for my phone.

"Hey. You said you're always here for me," I say. "Well… I need you now."

*

As I knock on the front door, I try to remember the last time I was here. I mentally sift through the years, settling on a random memory of me and Rob doing a drive-by visit one Christmas Eve. After handing over a bottle of wine in a gift bag covered with Santa faces, we sat down for a few awkward moments of faux holiday cheer. I recall praying that we had at least thirty minutes of conversation in us. We lasted for fifteen before the obligatory, rapid-fire catching up wound down into awkward silence.

"It's good to see you," he says. "Come on in."

"Thanks, Dad," I say. "It's good to be here."

I follow him into the living room, where Alice is putting down glasses of iced beverages on the coffee table.

"I hope lemonade is okay," she says. "It's all your father ever drinks."

"It's perfect," I say. "Thank you."

She moves toward me, and for a second I think she's going to hug me. But instead, she pats me lightly on the shoulders before gliding out of the room.

"I have to admit that I was surprised you called," he says. "But I'm glad you did." He takes a seat in an overstuffed chair, and I settle in on the couch across from him.

"Sorry it was so last minute," I say.

"Retirement has its benefits," he says. "I've got nothing but time." He takes a sip of his drink, waiting for me to continue.

"Rob and I are splitting up," I say. "It's my fault. I asked him for a divorce."

He lets out a long exhale. "Well, I'm truly sorry to hear that," he says. "But don't blame yourself. It takes two, you know."

"Yeah. But I feel like I completely blindsided him," I say. "And to be honest, I kind of shocked myself."

"How so?" he says. "You must've been thinking about this for a long time."

I look down at my hands. "I knew what I felt," I say. "I just didn't think it would ever come out of my mouth."

"But it did," he says. "And I'd imagine it's a relief."

"It is, in a way," I say. "But he's a good man. We have a history. And he just got a promotion that would have us living this freaking dream life in London. Any woman would be thrilled beyond belief, but all I wanted to do was run. What the hell is wrong with me?"

110

"Nothing," he says. "And there was nothing wrong with your mother, either."

"What do you mean?" I say.

"I was a good husband, in a provider sort of way," he says, taking a sip of his drink. "And I know Beth loved me, just as you do Rob. But it wasn't enough. She needed more. Someone who would share her dreams."

I feel my breath catch, wondering if he knew about Daniel. "You mean her writing?"

He nods. "I knew she played around with stories in her head," he says. "But I thought that was all it was. *Playing.* Something to keep herself amused."

"But it was more than that to her," I say.

"I didn't understand it. And I suppose I didn't care to, at the time," he says. "But when she came home and told me she'd gotten a job at Encanto, that's when I knew." He falls silent, swirling the ice cubes around in his glass.

"Knew what?" I say.

"That I was losing her," he says. "But I was stubborn. And stupid. She wanted me to encourage her; to say I was proud."

"But you wouldn't," I say. "Why?"

"I won't make excuses for myself," he says. "But the status quo is a powerful thing. Deceptive in the comfort it provides. Or that you hope it will, anyway."

"And sometimes you come to cherish it more than the person you claim to love," I say. "You don't even realize it's happening."

"Or you don't want to admit that it is," he says, giving me a long look. "It's a scary thing, letting go of a life you know so well."

"But I'm more afraid of who I'll become if I stay," I say. "Or who I'll never be."

"That's probably what Beth would've said if she thought I would've listened," he says, a tiny smile tugging at his lips. "I hated being alone. Because that's when you can't deny all the things you probably need to change about yourself."

"But you didn't want to change," I say.

"I didn't know how to," he says. "So, I found someone who allowed me to stay the same."

"Maybe Rob will find his Alice," I say.

He shrugs. "Right now, he's hurting. Just like I was," he says. "But he'll make a new start. And it'll be better for both of you."

"I just wish he saw it that way," I say. "A part of me wants to run back home and tell him I temporarily lost my mind. That I didn't mean anything I said."

"But you won't," he says. "Because you're being called for something more. And if you don't move toward it now, you never will."

I nod, feeling my eyes begin to fill up. My dad then does something he hasn't done since I was a little girl. He sits down next to me and pulls me close, letting my tears fall all over his perfectly pressed shirt.

And then he whispers the sweetest words I've ever heard him say.

"You are your mother's daughter, Charlotte. And I love you."

Chapter Twenty

"I'll take a large dark roast, and I'm paying for hers, too."

I turn around to see Will in line behind me at Cinnamon's, handing the barista a twenty-dollar bill before I can stop him.

"What are you doing here?"

"Well, you don't answer texts anymore," he says. "But I know you mainline coffee like a fiend every morning. Figured this is where you'd be."

"Seek, and ye shall find," I say. "Especially when there's caffeine involved."

We grab our drinks off of the counter, and Will follows me to a table. "Were you ever going to tell me you resigned?" he says. "Or just disappear and hope I wouldn't notice?"

"Look, I wasn't thinking about you or anyone else when I did it," I say. "All I knew was that I needed to get out of there."

"But why the big rush?" he says.

"Because there's just too much going on in my life right now," I say. "I need some time to process it all without everyone at the office trying to 'help.'"

"Shit," he says. "Trina told you."

"Yes, she did," I say.

"So, you quit because I overstepped my bounds," he says. "Why didn't you just talk to me?"

"About what?" I say. "The fact that you were right about me and Rob falling apart? Congrats on your conjugal radar, counsel."

"I'm sorry, Char," he says. "I know you don't believe me, but I am."

I nod. "So, how are things going with you and Shelly?" I say. "I'm guessing you've got Erica on the case."

"When you're going through a shit storm, you need the best," he says.

"I'll give her that," I say. "Wouldn't want to be within fifty miles of any court-room she's in."

"So, what are you doing next?" he says. "You got another gig lined up?"

"No, thank God," I say. "I'm done with the cube farm."

"Good for you," he says. "I mean it. And once I get things squared away with child support and the new post-split financial picture, I think I'm ready to make a change, too."

"Full-time photography?"

He nods. "I've still got my studio," he says. "You should see some of the stuff I'm working on. I think you'd like it."

"I'm sure I would," I say. "You're the real deal."

"Takes one to know one."

"I should probably get going," I say.

"Me, too," he says, looking like that is the last thing he wants to do. "I'll walk out with you."

Once we arrive at my car, he stops and turns to me. "Don't worry, I won't kiss you this time," he says. "But I can't make any future promises."

"Will…"

"You may never speak to me again after I say this, but I have to take my shot," he says. "You and I are going through something that not many other people could understand. Not just splitting from old loves, but returning to our first ones. The stuff we were put here to do. And I think it'd be a little bit crazy to not at least consider walking this path together."

"I hear you," I say. "It's just too soon."

"All right," he says, giving me a tiny smile. "But this is the last coffee ambush you'll get for a while."

"Fair enough," I say. "The next one's on me."

As he walks away, my heart thuds in my chest. I feel horrible for hurting someone I care so much about. But I know that as much as it would be comforting to lean on him, it would also be selfish. If I want what I say I do, then I have to be brave enough to go get it on my own.

It's time to hold my own hand.

*

"Phoebe, come on," I plead as she stares me down, refusing to evacuate the suitcase I'm trying to pack. "This is not a good day to mess with me." After a brief roll on her back to ensure that all my clothes are sufficiently coated with fur, she hops out and settles on the floor.

"Thanks for that," I say, grabbing a lint roller from the dresser and tossing it on top of my hairy garments. I glance at the bedside clock and see that it's almost six-thirty. Rob should be home soon, so I step up my pace, grabbing clothes, shoes, and toiletries and tossing them unceremoniously into my case.

"I've never seen you pack that fast in your entire life."

I turn to see Rob standing in the doorway, leaning against the jamb with his arms crossed. He looks more acquiescent and less angry than the last time I saw him, but he's clearly not happy with me.

"I was just trying to get some things together," I say, putting down the lid of the overfilled case and trying to smash it closed.

"You're going to break the latches," Rob says, nudging me aside and muscling it shut. "So, where are you running away to?"

"I'm going to stay with Abby for a while," I say. "Just until I figure out a place of my own."

"You don't have to leave," Rob says. "I know we're over, and I'm not fighting you. I just think it's stupid for you to squeeze into some crackerbox condo when we're perfectly capable of unraveling things like adults."

"Are we?" I say.

"If you're already out of love with me, what's the big deal about sharing space?" he says.

"It's not that simple, and you know it," I say.

Rob walks past me and sits on the bed. "I think you're afraid," he says. "You aren't as sure about this as you thought you were. So, now you've got to run like hell before you change your mind."

"I thought you weren't fighting me."

"I'm not," Rob says. "I'm questioning your decision one last time before it's too late for us to turn back."

"And what would we be turning back to?" I say. "I'm not being snide. I really want to know what you think we'd gain by staying together."

I can see him struggling to come up with an answer, so I press on. "Do I make you happy? Can you honestly say that you look forward to seeing me every day when you come home? Or are you just glad that someone—anyone—is there?"

"As usual, you're making this way too fucking complicated," he says.

"No, I'm not," I say. "So, just answer me. Please."

"Of course, I want someone to be there!" he says. "What's wrong with that?"

"Not a thing," I say. "But I don't want to be your marital white noise anymore. And I don't want you being mine."

"*Marital white noise?*" he says. "What crackpot guru did you get that one from?"

"I made it up myself," I say. "I think it's pretty good, actually."

"You're over-thinking us right into divorce court, you know."

"I'm sorry you feel that way," I say. "But one day—"

"Just stop," Rob says, holding up his hand. "I don't know how I'll feel 'one day.' Maybe I'll be as sure as you are that this is the right thing. But right now…"

I look over at Phoebe, who is glancing back and forth between us like she's watching a ping-pong match. She gets up, pads over to Rob and licks his hand a few times. She then meanders over to me and flops down, laying her head on my feet. Rob shakes his head, cracking an almost imperceptible smile as he reaches for my suitcase.

"I take it that Abby's condo association allows dogs."

Chapter Twenty-One

"Well, this is quite the spread," Daniel says as he watches me unpack bagels, cream cheese and a fruit plate from Cinnamon's. "Might even bring the appetite back."

"Let's hope so," I say, handing him his coffee. "Unlike the case for the rest of us, calories are your friends." Even dropping the chemo regime doesn't seem to have stopped his weight loss. He looks thinner than ever, and his skin is sallow and almost translucent.

"I figured once you had all my worldly secrets recorded for posterity, that'd be the last of you," Daniel says. "But I'm glad you're still coming around."

"Are you kidding? You're great company," I say. "And I think Mom would be happy that we became friends."

"I hope so," Daniel says. "As badly as I ruined my relationship with her, I really didn't deserve the chance to know her daughter."

"Don't say that," I say, reaching for a bagel and slathering it with cream cheese. "She wouldn't like that kind of talk, and neither do I." I push the loaded bagel toward him. "Eat."

"Aye, aye, Nurse Ratched," Daniel says, grinning as he obediently takes a bite. "Since my mother taught me never to talk with my mouth full, I guess it's your turn."

I start to speak but stop when I notice his smile fading as he looks past me toward the entryway of the kitchen. I turn around to see a small, dark-haired woman peering at us, her mouth pinched at the corners. Like Daniel, she's older now, and there is a good amount of gray mixed in with her carefully coiffed hair. But I remember her face from the *Los Angeles Times* piece Mom had saved.

"Hello, Claire," Daniel says. "I didn't think you'd be home so soon."

"Well, you were doing so horribly this morning, I thought I should come back," she says, clearly annoyed with the inconvenience. "You don't look any better. I don't know why you won't just see the doctor."

"This is Charlotte Grayson," he says, ignoring her icy barb. "I told you about her. She's writing my memoir."

"Nice to meet you," I say, extending my hand.

"And you, as well," Claire says, without shaking my hand. She turns to Daniel. "I'm going to sit outside and read. It's such a lovely day. No sense being cooped up in here, right?"

Daniel doesn't answer as she grabs a magazine from the kitchen table and heads toward the patio. He stays quiet, all the light gone from his eyes.

"She seems, um…"

"Don't bother struggling with pleasantries," Daniel says. "Especially when trying to explain someone so clearly unpleasant."

I nod in agreement, and he continues. "So, where were we?" he says, biting into his bagel again.

"Actually, there's one more thing I want to ask you about including in the book. But I don't think you know that it happened," I say. "I didn't. Not until I talked to Marnie."

Daniel nearly chokes. "You talked to her?"

"I *saw* her," I say. "I read something in one of Mom's journals about 'the secret that only Marnie knew.' I had to find out what it was. So, I took a road trip to Santa Barbara."

"You went to the Dolphin," he says.

"Dropped in without letting her know I was coming," I say. "But she was very gracious, once she got over her shock. She'd never met me, and she had no idea Mom had died."

"Well, you certainly make a grand entrance," he says. "So, did you find out the secret?"

"Yes," I say. "And I'm afraid to tell you because it's not good."

"I've been hit with just about everything of late," he says. "One more punch to the head won't do me in."

"Mom had a miscarriage, Daniel," I say. "It was your baby."

Daniel's face turns ashen. "Oh, my God," he says. "That can't… there's no way…"

"It's true," I say. "I wish it wasn't. Maybe I shouldn't have told you…"

"No, no. I'd rather know," he says, struggling to compose himself. "When did it happen?"

"It was the weekend you canceled on meeting her at the Dolphin," I say. "Because of the book awards ceremony in New York."

Daniel's jaw clenches, and I can see a small vein pulsing in his forehead. I'm about to ask if he's all right when he leaps out of his chair with more vigor than I've seen since I met him. "Stay here," he says. "I'll be right back."

I do as I'm told while he marches out to the patio where Claire is sitting. But as soon as I hear him raise his voice, I'm up and running toward the patio, too. I hang back enough that they can't see me, but I can hear every word between them.

"I'm leaving town for a while," Daniel says.

"That is ridiculous," Claire says. "You're sick, you crazy old fool."

"Yes, I'm sick. I'm old. And I'm definitely a fool," he says. "But not for the reason you think."

"Oh, believe me, I can think of plenty of reasons," she says.

"I'm a fool—and a coward—for letting you keep me from the woman I loved," he says. "You may have forgotten what you did, but I never have. And I never will."

"So, after all this time, you're going to go and be with her?" she says, a smirk tingeing her voice.

"She's dead, Claire," he says. "I just found out. And I'm going back to where I spent time with her. To the only place I ever really felt loved."

"What do you suppose your boys will think of you?" she says. "Running out on me like this, and putting your health in danger over the memory of some whore? What was her name… Beth?"

It's all I can do to keep from charging out there and giving that brittle old bitch a piece of my mind. Thankfully, Daniel continues before I do something stupid.

"I have no idea what they'd think, Claire. But they are grown men, not boys," he says. "And I suspect that by now they've lived long enough to have made plenty of their own shitty, regretful decisions. I'd like to think they'd forgive me for trying to make something right that's been wrong for a very long time."

"Well, we'll see about that," she says.

"I'm following my heart this time," he says. "Something you'd understand if you had one."

I realize too late that their conversation is over, and Daniel comes back into the house to catch me eavesdropping like a guilty kid. He doesn't seem to mind. Instead, he points toward the back bedroom.

"I'm going to throw some things together," he says. "And then you're driving me to Santa Barbara."

*

After a quick call to Abby to let her know that Phoebe will most likely be the sole guest in her condo tonight, Daniel and I are headed up the coast. He's lost in thought, so I try to let him relax while I drive. But there's something I heard in his conversation with Claire that keeps elbowing its way to the front of my mind.

"If you don't want to tell me, it's okay," I say. "But what did Claire do to you that you said you'd never forget?"

Daniel lets out a long exhale. "It's a bit of a story," he says.

"And we've got a long drive," I say.

"Remember when I told you that I worked as an editor at Encanto?" he says.

I nod, and he continues. "Well, what I didn't mention was that Claire's family owned the company."

"Holy shit," I say, feeling my stomach twist.

"After Claire had our first son, she became even more insistent that she not work," he says. "And to her way of thinking, my writing was just some sort of lark that took me away from the real business of making money for our family. So, she pulled some strings with her father and got me the editor job. I didn't want to do it, but I made a deal. I said that I'd take the job if she would guarantee me that Encanto would consider my writing for publication."

"So, did that make her happy?" I say.

"Her being pleased with anything I did would've been the first sign of Armageddon," he says. "But I hung in there to keep the peace. And I kept writing. Even more so after I met your mother. She inspired me like no one else ever has."

"Marnie told me that *Wheelhouse* was about you and Mom," I say. "How did Claire feel about you writing a story about a man who leaves his family for another love?"

Daniel smirks. "She thought so little of my work that she never even read the damn thing," he says. "That is until the other editors and agents fell in love with it. This pissed her off at first. But then she decided she liked the idea of being the wife of the latest literary golden boy."

"And that was the end of you and Mom," I say.

"Not right away," he says. "She knew how I felt about Beth, but I think she figured it would peter out. And when it didn't, she got angry. And then she got even."

"What do you mean?"

120

"When I told her I was skipping the book awards ceremony in New York, she was livid," he says. "She told me that she wasn't above having her father fire me and cancel my publishing contract. That there were plenty of one-hit wonder novelists, and chances are I was going to be one of them without the support of Encanto behind me."

"And you believed her."

Daniel stares out the window. "I can blame Claire all I want to for keeping me from Beth," he says. "But in the end, the choice was mine. And it's one I'll never forgive myself for."

I start to protest, but he holds up his hand. "I know we met under the guise of you writing my story," he says. "And I know you'll do a wonderful job with it. But there's something I care far more about."

"What's that?" I say.

"You writing your own story," he says. "And I don't mean a book. I'm talking about your *life*."

I feel a tear slide down my cheek as he continues. "You're just like me, Charlotte. You've done an excellent job of living everyone else's idea of a neat and tidy tale. The right job. The right marriage. Pretty maids all in a row.

"But regret over a half-lived life has eaten away at me far more than this cancer ever could. And I need you to promise me that from this point on, you'll concentrate on dismantling the perfect, the safe, and the sane. Write yourself one goddamned beautiful mess of an existence. Do you hear me?"

I'm crying too hard to answer, so I just nod. His face softens into a gentle smile, and he gives my arm a squeeze.

"One last thing," he says. "No editing allowed."

*

When we pull into the Dolphin's parking lot, I can feel Daniel brighten. He smiles and points toward the entrance, where a woman is walking with a large armful of cut flowers.

"My God," he says. "Is that Marnie?"

"It is," I say. "You want to go say hello?"

"I'm so damn ancient, she won't even recognize me," Daniel says, practically bounding out of the car.

"You may be old, but you can still pull off a wind sprint when you want to," I say, quickening my step to keep up with him.

As we get closer to Marnie, she waves, recognizing me instantly. I can see her squinting at Daniel, trying to figure out who he is.

"How are you, sweetie?" she says. "I'd give you a hug, but I've kinda got my hands full."

"Here, let me," Daniel says, taking the flowers from her. She thanks him and turns to embrace me.

"So, who's your friend?" she says, nodding toward Daniel.

"See? I told you she wouldn't remember," Daniel says, grinning at me.

"Okay, what's going on?" Marnie says, her eyes darting back and forth between Daniel and me.

"This is Daniel Jameson," I say.

"Well, I'll be damned," she says, her eyes narrowing. "Long time, no see."

Daniel's sunny demeanor dims. "I guess I shouldn't have expected you'd want me here," he says. "I just…"

"I told him about Mom's miscarriage," I say.

Marnie stares at me, shaking her head. "Why now, after all this time?"

"Charlotte is writing my memoir," Daniel says. "But it's not just about me anymore. It's *our* story. Mine and Beth's."

"Well, aren't you both just full of surprises," Marnie says, giving me a sideways glance.

"All I want is to take a look around the grounds one last time," Daniel says. "Relive some old memories. Pay some respects that are far too little, far too late."

Marnie's face softens as she takes the flowers back from Daniel. "Let me go put these in water," she says. "Then I'll go with you. I could use a little break."

*

Once we get started on the tour of the grounds, I can tell that Marnie's "little break" is going to stretch into several hours. But I don't think any of us mind. As Daniel begins to relive his memories, I watch as the years fall away from his bent and broken body. He stands straighter, moving with a quiet strength. When he smiles, I can see the light that drew my mother in all those years ago.

As he looks over at the pool, a tear slides from his eye. "That was Beth's favorite place," he says, wandering off towards it. I start to follow him, but Marnie puts her hand on my arm, gently holding me back.

"You really love him, don't you?"

122

I nod. "All I wanted at first was to know who he was. Why he meant so much to Mom," I say. "I never expected that he'd come to matter so much to me, too."

"I was angry at him for disappearing," Marnie says. "Mainly because he hurt your mother. But I cared about him, too. I thought he was my friend."

"He still is. And I'm glad he's here again to prove that to you," I say. "But you were right that it wasn't just some ego trip about the awards that kept him from ever coming back here." As I proceed to tell Marnie about Claire and her family's involvement in Encanto, her face pales.

"Well, goddamn," she says. "Makes perfect sense now. All those times I tried reaching him through his office. Not even a call back from an assistant."

"He was on lockdown," I say. "But not anymore. You should've seen him light into Claire when she told him he was a fool for coming here."

"He's a quiet one," Marnie says. "But those are the ones you've got to watch out for."

"I think it was good for him to get angry," I said. "He hasn't had that kind of energy in months."

"How's he doing?" Marnie asks. "I mean, do the doctors think he's going to make it?"

"He stopped treatment," I say.

"I don't blame him," Marnie says, motioning toward the pool where Daniel is stretched out on a chaise lounge, napping. "He needs to enjoy the time he has left."

"Guess that's true for all of us," I say. "Come on. Let's go check on Sleeping Beauty."

Daniel's eyes flutter open as he hears us approach. "Haven't napped so soundly in ages," he says, stretching as he sits upright. "It feels wonderful."

"I think it's the ocean breeze we get up here," Marnie says. "I call it 'Nature's Ambien.'"

"It's more than that," Daniel says. "It's her. She's everywhere."

"I know," Marnie says, putting her hand on his shoulder.

"Our child would be grown by now," he says. "But I can't help but think of all the times we could have shared this place with him or her."

"But you're here now," I say. "For the three of you."

"And I'm grateful," he says, looking at both me and Marnie. "Thank you for bringing me home again. In more ways than you'll ever understand."

Chapter Twenty-Two

"How'd you sleep?" Marnie says, handing me a cup of coffee as I enter the kitchen. Her staff is hustling to prepare for the brunch crowd, and I try to stay out of their way.

"Like a darted rhino," I say. "Has Daniel come down yet?"

"No. I figured he'd want to sleep in," Marnie says. "We were up pretty late last night."

"It was his fault," I say. "He's quite a talker."

"And pretty handy with a corkscrew, too," Marnie says. "How many bottles of wine did we knock off?"

"I don't do math before noon," I say. "I think I'm gonna go check on him. We've got to get on the road before too long."

I make my way up to Daniel's room and knock. After a few moments, there's still no answer.

"Hey, Daniel," I say through the door. "Come on, open up. Time for breakfast."

He doesn't respond, so I call him on my cell. I can hear it ringing inside the room until it finally goes to voicemail. My heart begins to thud in my chest as I race back down to the kitchen.

"Do you have a duplicate key for Daniel's room?" I say, forcing my voice to hold steady. "I can't get him to answer the door."

Marnie gives me an anxious look. "Let me get it," she says. "I'll go with you."

"No, that's okay," I say. "I'm sure he's just sleeping off last night's festivities. I don't want him to be embarrassed."

"All right," she says. "Be right back."

After she returns with the key, I practically sprint back to Daniel's room. The door opens easily, and I call out before I enter.

"Daniel? It's me," I say. "I'm sorry to let myself in, but you didn't answer."

I see him on the bed, lying on his side with his back turned toward me. *He's sleeping. Don't startle him.*

As I get closer, I listen for his breath, watching for any sort of rise and fall of his chest. I circle around the bed to face him, kneel down and put my hand on his cheek.

"Daniel," I whisper. "Wake up. Please."

But I can feel an unnatural coolness to his skin. His eyes are half closed, in a sort of limbo between waking and slumber. I put my face close to his, and feel nothing coming from his mouth. I shake him once, gently, just to be sure.

"No..." I whisper. "You can't..."

In my stupor, I somehow manage to call 911, tell them where I am, and what has happened. I phone downstairs to Marnie to warn her that paramedics are on the way, and to ask that she give me time alone with him until they arrive.

As the sobs tear through my body, I brush back the hair from his eyes and plant a soft kiss on his forehead. I remember the day in the hospice when Mom said goodbye. The day at the beach when I released her ashes to the sea and her pain to the wind. The afternoon when Jana gave me the box that would be the key to understanding what my mother's life was all about, and to finding out what mine was to become.

As I hear the sirens whine in the distance, I look at my friend one last time, and say the only words my heart has to offer:

"Full sails, Daniel... go with God."

*

As I drive back from Santa Barbara, I feel a little guilty for secretly hoping Abby won't be home when I get there. She was incredibly supportive of Operation Find Daniel, but right now I don't have it in me to tell the story of his passing to anyone but Phoebe.

Just as I reach for my cell to turn it off in hopes of a peaceful drive, it begins to chime in my purse. It's still in hands-free mode so I can see on my dash display that it's Quinn calling. I consider sending him to voicemail, but I know we have to talk. As Daniel's best friend, there will never be an easy time for him to hear the news.

"Hey, Quinn," I say. "How are you?"

"Confused," he says. "I just got a call from Daniel's wife. That alone is strange enough because she and I aren't exactly the best of friends."

125

"So, what's her problem?" I say.

"She said that Daniel went crazy on her," he says. "Told her he was going out of town. Then she said that 'some young woman who is writing a book with him' threw him in the car and took off with him."

"She certainly has a flair for the dramatic," I say. "I didn't *throw* him anywhere. I was just the chauffeur. He was going to go whether I took him or not."

"Where'd you go?" Quinn asks.

"The Delinquent Dolphin," I say. "I overheard you talking about it in the store, when Daniel didn't make it to the signing."

Quinn is silent for a moment, and I can hear him catch his breath. "Are you still up there?" he says.

"No, I'm on my way back home," I say.

"What about Daniel?" he says. "Is he with you?"

"No, he's…" I say. "He passed away. I'm so sorry. I found him this morning in his room."

"Oh, my God…"

"It just looked like he was sleeping," I say. "I think he went peacefully."

"At least he was someplace that felt like home," Quinn says. "He deserved that much."

"I should've called you sooner," I say. "I just didn't have it in me."

"I understand," he says, his voice breaking. "I can't wrap my head around never seeing him again."

"Me neither," I say. "I know I haven't known Daniel nearly as long as you have. But the time we had together was more than just a chance to write about some literary legend. He became my mentor and my friend. I really came to love him."

"I know you did. And he felt the same way," Quinn says. "He told me who you are."

"I can explain…"

"You don't have to," he says. "When I first met you, I thought you didn't seem like a real journalist to me. Wasn't sure I should put you two in touch."

"But you did," I say. "Why?"

"Couldn't put my finger on it," he says. "I told myself that Daniel needed the publicity if he was gonna get back in the game. But I think a part of me knew he needed a friend even more. Someone besides me to talk with."

"Thank you, Quinn," I say. "For sharing your friend with me."

"Don't be a stranger, okay?" he says. "I think Daniel would've liked for us to stay in touch."

"I think so, too," I say. "I'll stop by the store soon."

"Please do," Quinn says. "There's something I've been meaning to talk to you about. Might be good for both of us."

One Year Later

"So, are you nervous?" Quinn says.

"Are you kidding?" I say. "I'm scared shitless! What if no one shows up?"

"Well, they'd better," he says, grinning. "Look how many of these suckers I have to unload!" He motions toward a display table laden with copies of Daniel's memoir, *Waiting to Wake: A Life on Hold*.

"I still can't believe I'm having a signing next week," I say.

"Well, get ready, girl," Katya says, grinning as she flips through one of the books. "I'm bringing the entire Scribe Tribe with me and they all want autographed copies for friends and family. You'll probably end up with carpal tunnel."

"From your mouth to God's ears," Quinn says. "Well, not the carpal tunnel part."

"You know, I wouldn't even be published if you hadn't twisted your friend's arm at Encanto," I say.

"Didn't take much convincing," Quinn says. "It's a great story, and Daniel was one of their brightest stars. They'd have been fools to pass on it."

"I just wish he was here to see this," I say. "Mom, too."

Quinn puts his arm around my shoulder and gives it a squeeze. "I know you're a big shot author and all, but it's time to get back to the grind." He smiles, motioning toward a gaggle of customers that have just walked in the door.

"You got it, boss," I say, turning to make my way toward the group.

I've been working for Quinn at the store ever since I got back from Santa Barbara after Daniel died. It's the best job I've ever had. I'm not making the money I did at the firm, but cashing out my 401K has definitely helped supplement things. I know, I know… it's a dicey move at my supposedly advanced age, and several people have politely reminded me of that. But safety and security are about as illusory as a unicorn; and in a race between the three, I'd put my money on the one-horned beast every time. At least it farts rainbows.

But I'm happy and grateful to finally be living a life that feels like a second skin, instead of some ill-fitting office ensemble. I wanted to love corporate life, and God knows Rob has reaped his rewards from it. If I'd stayed with him, I could have, too. But we are both where we should be: me here with Phoebe, and him living the life of an honorary Englishman abroad. We haven't talked in a while, and I don't know if or when we will since the divorce has been finalized. But I really do wish only the best for him. He deserves all that we couldn't give each other, and then some. And if that sounds cheesy, too bad. It's how I feel, and I don't edit myself much these days.

I still miss Daniel all the time. Just like with Mom, sometimes I feel his presence. Other times, it seems like I'll never connect with either of them again. I'm afraid to forget the sound of their voices or to lose any one of the small vignettes I play over and over, hoping to wear a permanent groove in my mind's eye.

In those moments, I tell myself that they haven't gone missing. They are simply—and joyously—preoccupied because they've found each other once more. Experiencing their love in a place where it can't be corralled by limits or judgment, or smothered by secrecy and heartbreak. I picture them creating stories and poetry together. So many volumes that the heavens can't hold them, and there is no choice but for their words to spill down from the skies. Creative manna for anyone lucky enough to collect it.

And then I take out my notebook and begin to write.

41735470R00081

Made in the USA
Columbia, SC
15 December 2018